That Special Someone

TANYA BULLOCK

blackbird

Published by Blackbird Digital Books 2015

ISBN-9780993307003
Cover design by Darren Lewis

PART ONE
IZZIE & JAYA

'When you are a mother, you are never really alone in your thoughts. A mother always has to think twice, once for herself and once for her child.'

Sophia Loren

Prologue

mother and daughter

Izzie: I have very little memory of the night Jaya was conceived. In the weeks and months that followed, the vague recollections I did have were so surreal and sexy that, had it not been for the gradual expansion of my waistline, I might have attributed them to some bizarre erotic dream. Now, almost twenty years on, even those hazy memories have faded; like ancient coffee-coloured photographs with gently curling edges, the specific detail is blurry and soft. Strangely however, a few snapshots from that evening have become imprinted on my mind in startlingly sharp focus. I remember a picture-perfect sunset, two empty bottles of Cobra Beer in the sand, the smell of fried fish, the dopey, plodding cow which blundered a path through our love-making (I wish I could forget the cow!), the Arabian Sea before me, the gritty taste of sand in my mouth – and him: an outline moving in the shadows, a supple and angular body, a hungry mouth on my neck, an intoxicating scent of coriander and cologne. My daughter's father is nothing more to me than a collection of random memories and yet, on the rare occasions when I permit myself the luxury of steamy thoughts, I always think of him.

Jaya: I live with my mum in Netherton. Netherton is a good place to live because it's next to Merry Hill, which is my favourite place in the whole world. Merry Hill is probably the biggest shopping centre in England and I go there nearly every Saturday with my mum. Mum is white, but I'm only half white. My other half is Asian. I've never met my dad, but mum says he's from India. I've never been to India, but I've got lots of pretty saris, which is what Indian ladies wear. I don't have any other family, apart from my grandparents, who I've never met because they're racist.

Izzie: I've always had a high tolerance of parental disapproval. At some point in my early childhood I reached two important conclusions: a) that it was unrealistic I would ever become my mother and father's ideal daughter and, b) that it didn't actually bother me. Life was much simpler after that. When, at sixteen, I informed them that I would no longer be accompanying them to church every Sunday, I endured the ensuing torrent of criticism and condemnation with calmness and composure. When I came home with a nose-ring at the age of seventeen, my parents didn't speak to me for over a month and I enjoyed the peace and quiet. Similarly, when at eighteen, I dropped out of college and hopped on a plane to India, I did so with full peace of mind. Upon my return a year later, I faced my parents' wrath with my usual sang-froid before serenely dropping another bombshell: I was four months pregnant. Incensed, they invoked God the Father, the Son and the Holy Spirit to rain down upon my head a plague of locusts, pestilence and venereal disease (or words to that effect). I was a whore, a Jezebel, an ingrate, a wayward slut of a daughter, a source of intense mortification and shame. I accepted all insults

2

with grace and good humour, picked up my backpack and left.

My inherent immunity to the opinions of my parents remained intact until Jaya was born. From then on, all that mattered to me was what was best for her, which presented me with somewhat of a predicament: how did a selfish, conceited teenager with no partner or real friends, no money, no qualifications and no home, go about providing a stable upbringing for her infant daughter? For the first time in my life, I needed my parents. I felt sure I could rely on their strong sense of duty; strict Catholics, they would undoubtedly forgive their prodigal daughter, slaughter the fatted calf and welcome their grandchild into the family fold. Admittedly, the signs were not good. I went through a lonely, complicated and painful childbirth at Russells Hall Hospital. Afterwards, the space around my bed on the maternity ward was conspicuously empty of well-wishers. As I lay there during the first few befuddling, bleary-eyed days of motherhood, I was aware of other new mothers and their family members sneaking sympathetic glances in my direction. When I was released from hospital, I returned to the women's hostel where I had spent the last four months of my pregnancy and, apart from an endless stream of concerned health professionals, I had no other visitors. For six months I did nothing but care for my baby and re-evaluate my life. I eventually managed to convince Social Services (and myself!) that I was a fit mother and emerged from my self-imposed solitary confinement a responsible adult. I was ready to face my parents.

One bitter morning in January 1995 found me, babe in arms, standing on the front porch of my parents' austere white semi. Trembling with cold and nervous anticipation, I took my courage in both hands and rang the bell. The door opened and the familiar form of my mother appeared before me. As I searched her eyes for a glimmer of maternal feeling, I was rewarded with the weakest of smiles. My hopes soared as I held Jaya up for her to see. My mother peered at her grandchild over her glasses.

'She's very dark-skinned,' she said.

'Her father is Indian,' I replied, my hopes of reconciliation squeezed as flat as the thin line of my mother's lips.

'*Indian?*' she said, as she might have said '*Martian*?'

'Oh, for Christ's sake!' I snapped.

The whiteness around my mother's tightly closed mouth spread to the rest of her face.

'*Do not* take the Lord's name in vain!'

Her hypocrisy stunned me into silence.

'If you're going to come in, do it quickly,' she hissed. 'I don't want the neighbours knowing your shameful little secret.'

I looked at her and, in that moment, understood why for all those years I had so systematically rejected her values and shunned her approval.

'Good-bye, mother,' I said as I turned to walk away. She didn't try to stop me. That was the last I ever saw of her.

Jaya: I go to college three days a week to do a Skills For Life And Work course and Functional Skills, which are English, Maths and ICT. I like English, but I don't like Maths or ICT. Maths is hard because you have to learn about money, which means you have to add up the things you want to buy, then hand over the right coins and then count your change. I like buying things, but I'm not always sure what each coin means. Mum lets me buy one thing every time we go to Merry Hill. Usually I buy nail-varnish or lipstick. My favourite colour lipstick is Autumn Apple because browny-red is the hue which best complements my skin-tone. I found that out on the internet. I know a lot about make-up. My mum never wears it because she says she's beautiful enough. I tell her she should wear foundation because she's quite old and has wrinkles. She says I'm a cheeky wench. She makes me laugh. My mum is my favourite person in the whole world.

Izzie: My tiny daughter entered the world on a sweeping wave of change which engulfed me, overwhelmed me and spilt over into every area of my existence. The woman who holds her child for the first time is never the same woman who conceived that child. Her body, lifestyle, clothes, dreams and future plans will all have been altered to some lesser or greater degree. Personally, my initial response to motherhood was a full-blown identity crisis. I felt that, as I had given life to Jaya, she had taken mine. I lay in my hospital bed, the same three words whirling round my head: *Who am I?* Before Jaya, I could have answered this question in a flash: I was a loner, a firecracker, an adventure-seeker, a sex-bomb, a go-getter. Men wanted me. Women envied me. No more. I held my newborn in my arms, my sense of self in tatters. It was a bad case of the "baby blues". Luckily, my hormones soon settled down and my maternal instincts kicked in. I was flooded with love for my baby. It was a love like no other; it soothed my troubled mind, healed my aching body and filled the hole where "me" once was.

Jaya: My best friend at college is Kerry Holt. We're the prettiest girls on the Skills For Life And Work course – everyone says so. Kerry's boyfriend is called Ian Kennedy. I haven't got a boyfriend, which isn't fair because I'm actually a bit prettier than Kerry Holt. Kerry and Ian hold hands at lunchtime and sometimes they kiss when they think no-one's looking. I kissed a boy once at a Mencap disco. I had to sit on his lap because he was quite short, but I didn't mind because he was a *really* good kisser.

Izzie: I always knew that there was something wrong with Jaya. I knew it long before her paediatrician confirmed it. I knew it when she was eight weeks old and didn't respond to my voice ('All babies develop at their own pace,' the health visitor reassured me). I knew it when she was a toddler and constantly bit her hands in frustration ('It's the terrible twos,' my GP explained patiently). But I knew differently. I knew Jaya. When she turned three and still couldn't say 'mummy', my GP finally took me seriously and referred her to a paediatrician.

I took an instant dislike to Dr Moore. He was a bearded, condescending old dinosaur, who had so patently never been a child himself that I doubted he would have the first clue how to help my little girl. For her sake however, I banished my concerns, put on a brave face and took Jaya to see him on numerous occasions. Over the next year, Dr Moore tested for and ruled out various disorders and conditions with complex and frightening sounding names; Jaya didn't have autism, dyspraxia, Asperger's syndrome, Heller's syndrome or epilepsy. As each possible illness was crossed off his list, I became increasingly anxious. How could I support Jaya if I didn't know what was wrong? Then, on the day before her fourth birthday, Dr Moore informed me that he was discharging Jaya from his care.

'Have you found out what the problem is?' I asked him.

He nodded. 'Her delays in oral development, deficiency in memory skills and difficulty in processing new information all point to one obvious conclusion...'

I was on the edge of my seat. 'Yes...?'

'She has significantly impaired cognitive abilities.'

My heart hit the floor. It had taken twelve months for the pompous old fart to tell me what I already knew.

'Can't you be any more precise?'

'Not really,' he replied. 'Jaya doesn't have a diagnosable condition. These things happen. I can't do any more for her, I'm afraid.'

These things happen. His words rang in my ears. These things happen? That wasn't the answer I wanted! I shook my head in disbelief. There were still so many questions I needed answering. *These things happen.* How? Why? How do you cope when they do?

a new teaching assistant

Izzie: Jaya's remarkably sprightly this morning. She seems really excited about going to college and spent much longer than usual on her hair and make-up. She even went to the effort of putting on her "party eyes"; a thick line of liquid mascara on each eyelid, topped with a smudge of glittery eye shadow.

'Anything special happening at college today?' I ask her over breakfast.

'No,' she replies, stuffing a spoonful of cornflakes into her mouth.

'Then why the "party-eyes" and the chignon?'

I can tell she's not even listening to me. Her eyes are on the kitchen clock and she's practically hovering over her chair.

'It's quarter-past-eight,' she says, proudly.

'Well done,' I say. It's actually quarter-to, but I don't want to dampen her new found enthusiasm for telling the time. 'Now sit down properly and eat your breakfast.'

She reluctantly pulls her chair closer to the table.

'Now,' I continue, 'what's the big rush and why are you all dolled up?'

At that moment the doorbell rings.

'Ring & Ride!' she exclaims as she jumps up from her chair. 'Bye mum. Love you.'

She blows me a kiss and is gone. As soon as I hear the door slam, I reach for the phone and dial Bee's number. Kishan answers the phone with his customary heavy breathing and suppressed giggles. In the background, I can hear Bee telling him he's going to be late for the day centre.

'Day centre... day centre... DAY CENTRE!' he bellows into the receiver. I hold the phone at arm's length; Kishan has a *very* loud voice. After a short struggle, I hear him relinquish the phone to his mother.

'You're through to Bina's Madhouse. Admissions department. How can I help you?'

No matter how bleak I'm feeling, Bee can always make me smile.

However, this morning I'm in no mood for light-hearted chitchat. I quickly tell her about Jaya leaving for college dressed like Paris Hilton.

'Do you think there's a boy involved?' she asks.

'There could be,' I reply. 'Do you think I should be worried?'

Bee falls silent. I know she's considering how best to advise me.

'If I was you,' she says eventually, 'I wouldn't be overly concerned. So what if she does have a boyfriend? She *is* eighteen.'

I suppress a groan and close my eyes. In my head I see a montage of romantic moving images: Jaya and boyfriend holding hands at the pictures, Jaya and boyfriend sucking on either end of the same strand of spaghetti, Jaya and boyfriend sitting on a park bench... he whispers something in her ear... she giggles... he leans in to kiss her... my eyes snap open.

'I just don't think she's ready, that's all,' I say.

'Of course you don't,' laughs Bee. 'You're her mum.'

Bee's insouciance does nothing to lighten my mood and I remain sullenly silent. On the other end of the line, Bee sighs and changes tack. 'Cheer up, sweetie,' she says, 'you know what Jaya's like about her appearance. She's probably just trying out a new beauty technique she's seen on *Gok's Fashion Fix*.'

As I hang up, I feel relief wash over me. Bee's right; Jaya's probably just experimenting with a different look. Nothing new there. I laugh at my own paranoia. There's no point getting my knickers in a twist every time Jaya dons a new sari or curls an eyelash!

Jaya: There's a new teaching assistant at college. His name is John and he's *so* sexy. I can't wait to get to college today to see him again. I think I'm in love!

Izzie: After filling my head with nonsense, I now feel an urgent need to clear it. I pull on my overcoat and head out into the murky morning. As I close the front door, I'm reminded of how much I used to hate that it led straight from the living room onto the street. I don't mind so much now. Now that I know where to find all the local hidden gems, the unruly youths and swirling crisp-packets barely even register. In half an hour I can be tramping the towpaths of Dudley Number 2 Canal, or bimbling through Bumble Hole, or admiring the cliffs of Doulton's Claypit. I set a brisk pace – a luxury I can only afford when I walk alone, as I've never met anyone who can keep up with me. I walk up Hill Street, passing St. Andrew's Church, which is one of my favourite haunts. For some reason, browsing the inscriptions on eroding gravestones has a calming effect on my soul. But not today. Today my soul needs water and so I head over the crest of Netherton Hill and begin my descent towards Lodge Farm Reservoir.

Jaya: John isn't at the bus stop to meet me this morning which is actually quite annoying because I've spent ages on my hair and make-up. Maggie's there instead and she smiles and says good morning. I say good morning back but it isn't really a good morning because Maggie's at the bus stop instead of John. Maggie walks us all into college from the bus stop and I buy a cup of tea from the cafeteria because it's still early and I've got ages yet until my first lesson. So I'm drinking my tea and minding my own business when suddenly there are two hands over my eyes and I know *for sure* they're John's from the lemon soap smell. Guess who? says John and I say Kerry as a joke which makes him laugh a lot. Then he sits down and he's so close to me that our shoulders are touching. He smiles and asks me if I'm OK and I'm so excited that I actually forget to breathe and I feel like I need a wee but I don't.

Izzie: I sit and take stock on a roadside bench, staring at the choppy waters of the former clay pit. Beyond the reservoir, Saltwells Wood is just about visible through the morning mist. I love this area; steeped in industrial history, once teeming with the workers from collieries, pits, quarries and mills, now reborn as quiet woodland and green open spaces. I breathe in the filmy air, thick with the secrets of this rich and ancient land. A car zooms past me and I catch a glimpse of an errant baseball-cap, facing backwards on its owner's head. A boy-racer, no doubt on his way to meet his yobbo mates for an illicit morning car-chase. I follow the foggy trail of exhaust fumes towards Merry Hill, with its enticing network of roads. It seems impossible to me that a shopping centre and a nature reserve can co-exist in such close proximity. But then that's the wonderful thing about living here; no matter how urban and built-up it may seem, there's always a rural idyll close by to escape to.

Jaya: This is the best day ever! I was eating my lunch with Kerry and Ian when John came over and sat by me *again*. He's sitting next to me now and smiles at me whenever he sees me looking at him. Usually when a boy keeps looking at me and smiling he ends up asking me out. I wonder if John wants to ask me out? I whisper this to Kerry and she laughs and says no way stupid. But Kerry's always been jealous of me so what she says doesn't count.

Izzie: I hug my coat to my body in an attempt to preserve the delicious melancholy of Saltwells Wood in the brooding fog. Bee passes me a sandwich and a mug of tea.

'The heating is on, you know,' she says, her black eyes twinkling.

'What do you mean?' I ask her.

She motions towards my thick duffle coat. 'I know this old stable is a bit draughty, but it isn't *that* cold.'

I giggle at this wildly inaccurate description of her home. Everything in her snug terrace kitchen oozes effortless style, from the vintage mannequin bust by the window, to the bold Miró prints on the wall.

'What's up with you anyway?' she asks.

'Just a bit nostalgic,' I reply.

She rolls her eyes. 'Been skulking around the nature reserve again?'

Bee has the uncanny ability to read me like a book. It used to bother me, but not any more.

'All morning,' I chuckle. I put down my plate and give her a big bear hug. 'Do you remember the day we first met?' I ask her.

'Oh my life!' she exclaims. 'You were such a cow, I'm hardly likely to forget.'

I laugh out loud at this. She's right. I was a cow. It was in the playground of Jaya's primary school on her very first day. I was watching my little girl trot across the tarmac, surrounded by children with various disabilities; kids with Down's Syndrome, kids in mini-wheelchairs, kids hobbling on crutches, kids with guide canes, kids with hearing aids.

As I was waving Jaya a cheery goodbye, I was suddenly struck by the seeming unfairness of it all. All those tiny individuals were so diverse and unique, that it just didn't seem *right* to lump them together under the banner of "disability". That got me thinking. Where exactly did Jaya fit in? She didn't have a physical disability and her problems seemed relatively minor when compared to those of some of the little mites braving their way across the school playground. The more I studied Jaya's young classmates, the guiltier I felt over my decision to send her to a special school. As I stood there, I was suddenly ambushed by my old enemy, Panic, who fired questions into my brain, like painful, explosive little gunshots. *Is this the right environment for her? Will her specific needs be met? Will she fit in?* (If so, she might not be sufficiently stimulated and challenged.) *Will she feel lonely and alienated?* (If so, the experience could leave her traumatised and withdrawn.) I was just on the point of chasing dementedly across the playground and dragging Jaya back home, when I felt a friendly tap on my shoulder. I turned to see a vivacious-looking young Asian woman grinning chummily at me. She nodded towards the crowd of children.

'Which one's yours?' she asked.

I pointed at Jaya.

'The Asian girl?'

'Mixed race,' I corrected.

'Of course. So... you're married to an Asian?' she enquired.

I shook my head, but offered no further explanation.

'Divorced? Widowed?' she persevered.

'No,' I replied abruptly, hoping she'd get the message and bugger off. However, the woman seemed undaunted by my frostiness and continued to smile affably at me.

'So... she's adopted then?'

Her persistence astounded and infuriated me; the nosey cow could not take a hint!

'She's the product of a drunken one-night-stand, OK? Her father could have been black, brown or *blue* for all I knew or cared!'

I stared defiantly into her eyes, awaiting the inevitable shock and disgust. It never came. Instead, my future best friend threw back her head and laughed. Her mirth was genuine, warm and infectious and it melted my icy armour. I extended my hand, shyly.

'I'm Isabel.'

'Bina,' she said, still giggling, 'but you can call me Bee.'

I turn to Bee now. 'Fourteen years ago,' I sigh. 'Blimey... that's gone fast.'

She puts her arm around me. 'You OK?' she asks. 'I was a bit worried this morning when you started going off on one.'

I shrug. What can I say? I never feel fully in control when it comes to Jaya.

'She'll be fine,' says Bee, reading my mind yet again.

'I hope so.' I give my best and only friend a kiss on the cheek and head for home.

Jaya: I wave good-bye to John from the steps of the Ring & Ride. Bye John I say and he says good-bye sweetheart. *Sweetheart*! That's what boyfriends say to their girlfriends. Now I know for sure John wants to be my boyfriend. I want to be his girlfriend too!

day trip

Jaya: Mum won't be up for ages yet so I've got lots of time to choose the perfect outfit. I'm really looking forward to the trip but the best thing is that John is going too. I hope we get to sit next to each other on the coach. I'm not sure whether to tell him yet that I want to be his girlfriend. Maybe I should wait until he asks to kiss me. Usually when a boy asks to kiss me I say no but I'll definitely say yes to John. What if he tries to kiss me today at the museum? I'd better wear my party clothes just in case.

Izzie: It's really early in the morning, but I can hear Jaya moving about her bedroom. I try to go back to sleep, but my curiosity gets the better of me. I slide from under the duvet, tiptoe across the landing and put my head around her door. I catch her staring at herself in the full-length mirror. She's fully dressed and her outfit is wholly inappropriate.

'You're not wearing *that* skirt or *those* heels to the Black Country Living Museum,' I tell her firmly. She jumps at the sound of my voice; I've clearly roused her from a deep reverie.

'Mum? Would you say I was beautiful, or just pretty?' she asks, turning back to the mirror.

'Pretty silly, if you ask me.' I cross to her wardrobe, pick out a sensible pair of jeans and a high-necked jumper and throw them on the bed. 'Get out of those ridiculous clothes... *now*!' I command.

'I am beautiful though, aren't I, mum?' she asks, as she steps out of her shiny mini-skirt. She looks at me imploringly with those huge Bambi eyes and I'm forced to concede. I nod. There's really no point denying it. She *is* beautiful. In fact, she's astoundingly beautiful and this is a huge cause of concern for me. Whenever I look into her eyes; two pools of liquid blue, striking against the creamy-brown, heart-shaped face in which they're set, I worry. I worry that she is neither responsible enough, nor wise enough to be in possession of such beauty. I worry that she will misuse and take advantage of it, or that, worse still, someone will misuse and take advantage of her because of it. Jaya finishes dressing in my chosen outfit and strikes a provocative pose in front of the mirror. I sigh, feeling defeated. That girl could make a coal sack look like a sexy little Prada number!

Jaya: We're on our way! The coach picked us up from college and drove past Merry Hill, which is my very favourite place in the whole world. I'd love to get a job on a make-up counter at Merry Hill, but Karen says you have to be good at maths to work in a shop, so I've got no chance. I ask Amanda if we can go to Merry Hill instead of the Black Country Living Museum, but she says no, we're going to the Black Country Living Museum and do you realise how much time and effort I've put into organising this trip? I don't mind though, because John is sitting next to me on the coach and there were loads of other people he could have sat next to. I can tell Kerry Holt is really jealous because she keeps giving me evils the whole time. I nearly tell her that me and John are in love but I don't because she would only say something nasty.

16

The Black Country Living Museum isn't like a proper museum, but has streets and houses and shops and stuff. Everything is really weird and old-fashioned, even the sweets, which are boiled and in big jars. We go into a lady's house and I feel a bit bad because we just go straight in without knocking. She's knitting by the fire and she smiles at us, so maybe she doesn't mind us all being in her living room after all. Then we go to an old school. The teacher's dressed in funny clothes and I feel sorry for her because maybe she can't afford to buy nice clothes. I always wear nice clothes because I'm pretty. The teacher shouts at us and tells us to stop talking. Then she asks to see Kerry Holt's fingernails and she tells her off because they're dirty. Kerry starts to cry and John puts his arm around her which is actually quite annoying because it's me he fancies not her. Then the teacher says sorry and tells Kerry that she's only an actress pretending to be a teacher from the olden days. I wouldn't mind being an actress one day but I wouldn't want to be an actress in a museum. I want to wear nice clothes like the dresses Katy wears on *Corrie*. Maybe I'll be an actress on *Corrie* or *Emmerdale*. Kerry Holt thinks the people in soaps are real. She cries when someone dies on telly. I told her once that they don't really die, but get up straight after and have a cup of tea and go home to their families. Kerry looked at me funny and said that wasn't true because when people die they get put in a coffin in the ground, like her Nan. Kerry Holt can be really stupid sometimes, even if she is my best friend. Mum says there's no such thing as stupid. She says that every person has different abilities and disabilities, which is why everyone is special and unique. I'm not sure what Kerry Holt's special abilities are, but mine are make-up and shopping. No college tomorrow, so I won't see John for a whole day.

That's twenty-four hours, which is a *really* long time to wait when you're in love!

Izzie: She's been in the bath for over an hour now. I can hear her singing some stupid pop song about being in love and everyone else being jealous. All that preening in front of the mirror this morning and now she's singing love songs in the bath... no prizes for guessing the reason! I knock on the bathroom door.

'Jaya, love, we need to talk.'

No answer, but the singing gets louder – her way of sticking two fingers up to me. I calmly make myself a cup of tea and lie in wait.

Jaya: I love One Direction almost as much as I love John. When I see them on YouTube or on TV it's like they're actually looking straight at me. Sometimes I think they write songs just for me and can read my mind or something. I mean how else would they know *exactly* how I feel about John?

Izzie: She saunters into her bedroom, wrapped in a towel, eyes half closed and humming that *ridiculous* song. When she eventually notices me sitting on her bed, she staggers backwards in surprise.

'Mum! What are you doing in my bedroom?'

'Waiting for you.'

'Why?'

I motion for her to sit next to me on the bed, but she remains standing, looking down on me with that exasperating, unreadable expression on her face.

'Jaya, I think we need to have a little chat about boys.'

'Oh not again, mum,' she whines.

'Yes *again*, Jaya! It's important.'

She grabs her fleecy pyjamas from the foot of the bed and yawns. 'I'm *sooo* tired, mum.'

I know there's no point carrying on this conversation. Jaya is a master of evasion when she wants to be. I stand and walk to the door.

'Night, mum. Love you,' she says.

I sigh. 'Love you too.'

If she thinks that's the end of it, then she's got another thing coming!

progression meeting

Jaya: I'm trying to think of a topic for my internet research project, but I'm finding it hard to pick one. Karen asks me what my very favourite thing is. I tell her that my very favourite thing is make-up. Karen says to go on the internet to do some research on make-up, but I say I don't need to because I already know everything there is to know about make-up. Karen says no-one knows everything about something and that I should go on the internet anyway. I don't mind though, because she asks John to help me. He sits *really* close to me and puts his hand on mine to help me with the mouse. Karen comes over and says that I only need help with reading and typing and that I can use the mouse on my own. When Karen goes away, I pretend I've forgotten how to use the mouse and ask John to show me what to do. John says OK, but don't tell Karen because it's our secret. He winks at me, which makes my tummy feel funny, but in a nice way. I've dreamed about this moment and now it's actually happening – John is touching me and it's *amazing*. My hand starts to tingle under his and I can feel my face going red. I start to get a really nice bubbly feeling between my legs and my breath gets stuck in my throat and then... then the door opens and in walks Mandy with... mum! At first I think I must be dreaming but mum really is here standing in the middle of my ICT class. Mum,

Mandy and Karen are all looking at me and I turn to John but he's moved to the next table and is busy helping Sam Cooper with his typing. Mandy points at me so I get up out of my seat. Then Karen tells the class to carry on with their internet research projects and walks towards the door. Me, mum and Mandy all follow her out.

Izzie: I try to catch Jaya's eye but she refuses to look at me, so I clear my throat and just come out with it.

'Does Jaya have a boyfriend at college?'

Both Amanda and Karen look uncomfortable and Jaya goes an unsightly shade of purple. I feel terrible for embarrassing her, but I *have* to know.

'Don't you think that's a question you should be asking Jaya?' suggests Karen.

'I've tried,' I say pointedly, glaring at my daughter, but she looks away.

Mandy smiles kindly at me. 'Not that it's any of my business, but I haven't noticed anything between Jaya and any of the male students.'

Jaya looks up at this. 'That's because I'm not going out with any of them,' she says, sullenly.

'Well, there's your answer,' says Karen.

Jaya: At least I didn't tell a lie. John *isn't* a student. I'll tell mum the proper truth soon, but I can't tell her in front of Mandy and Karen. Anyway, it's her fault if I didn't tell her about John because she shouldn't even be here. If she'd asked me at home then I would definitely have told her the truth. She's such a pain. I can't believe she's here. This is so embarrassing.

Izzie: Thank God for that. No boyfriend. I feel like a bit of an idiot now, but at least I've got the answer I wanted. I'm on the point of leaving when Karen grabs a folder from her desk.

21

'Actually, while you're here,' she says, 'we might as well make the most of it.'

Mandy nods. 'Yes, we're inviting parents and carers in for progression meetings.' She smiles cheerily. 'You've saved us the trouble.'

A progression meeting? I don't like the sound of this.

'A progression meeting?'

'Jaya completes her course in July,' explains Mandy, 'so we need to discuss what she's going to do next.'

This is completely out of the blue! I thought she'd get a bit more than two years out of the place. I try to remain calm. 'So, what are Jaya's options?' I ask.

'Well', replies Mandy enthusiastically, 'there's the local community centre. It runs Art Therapy classes.'

I can't *believe* I'm hearing this. Art *bloody* Therapy! That sounds like the sort of class you'd offer a child with a mental illness!

'Do you really think Art Therapy would be a step forward for Jaya?' I ask.

'Perhaps not,' concedes Karen. 'We should probably explore other avenues.'

'She likes make-up.' I suggest. 'You run Hair and Beauty courses here, don't you?'

Mandy looks embarrassed. 'Our Hair and Beauty courses start at level two,' she says, 'they're professional vocational qualifications.'

This conversation is starting to seriously annoy me.

'Jaya, what do *you* want to do?' asks Mandy diplomatically. 'Yes, let's ask Jaya,' agrees Karen.

All eyes turn to Jaya. She shrugs in that immensely irritating way of hers.

'Come on Jaya,' I urge, 'there must be something you want to do with your life?'

Jaya: We're supposed to be talking about me and what I want to do, but mum keeps telling Mandy and Karen what *she* thinks I should do. I quite liked the sound of art classes because I love painting and I think I'd enjoy it, but mum said no before I even had the chance to say anything. Now at last Mandy has asked what *I* want, but mum's acting like she thinks I don't want to do anything with my life, when I actually *do*. I know what I want, but I think it'll make mum even madder if I say it. I want to look after babies. I know I'd be really good at it because you don't need to be good at English or maths. You just need to cuddle them and give them milk when they cry. I could look after other people's babies, but it would be even better if I had my own baby. I'd love to have a baby to love and look after... and a husband too of course. I wonder if John would want to marry me? I think about how he held my hand and the way he looks at me and calls me sweetheart. Everyone's looking at me and I want to say it but I'm too embarrassed. What is wrong with you Jaya? says mum and that makes me so mad that I just come right out and say it.

Izzie: 'I want to get married,' says Jaya.

I'm so shocked that I actually do a double-take, like a dumbstruck character in a cartoon. *Married?* Who the hell to? She's just said she doesn't have a boyfriend. Karen laughs, relieved. She knows she's off the hook. 'I'm afraid we can't help you with that,' she says, smiling.

I shake my head. I can't deal with this right now.

'OK,' I say, trying to remain positive, 'so what *exactly* can you help her with?'

'Well,' begins Mandy, 'we have links to a wide network of support and care agencies. I could put you in touch with Mencap or I could give you the number for—'

'I'm quite capable of picking up the phone and ringing Mencap myself,' I interrupt. 'What I want to know is... where does Jaya go from here?'

Mandy looks uneasy and turns to Karen for support.

'The thing is,' says Karen firmly, 'this is an educational establishment, so when students achieve their qualifications, they leave. Jaya's been with us for two years and we feel she's reached her academic potential. It's time for her to move on and, as teachers, that's where our involvement ends.'

Case closed.

'Great. Well, thank you,' I say, standing up. 'You've both been very helpful! Your expert advice and guidance have really helped us steer Jaya in the right direction. I'm sure she's now fully equipped with the knowledge and information she needs to *progress*!' I spit out that last hypocritical word and storm out of the room.

Jaya: I follow mum out of the office but she's already gone. I go back to my ICT class but there's no-one in the room so the lesson must be finished. I don't really know what to do because usually John or Maggie or one of the other teaching assistants takes us from class to the bus. I think I know how to get to the main entrance but sometimes I get lost around college. It's really annoying because I've been coming here for ages so I should be able to find my way around but I can't. I start to get a sick feeling in my tummy because how will I get home if I miss the Ring & Ride? Then I see Maggie coming towards me and the sick feeling goes away. She smiles and says come on slow coach I've been looking for you. She puts her arm through mine and leads the way.

Izzie: I hate rain. I especially hate urban rain and Black Country urban rain is the worst rain of all. Big oily globules landing on car parks and boarded-up pubs. Grey skies closing in over grey streets; the dreary landscape discoloured to the point of almost post-apocalyptic bleakness. Why is there no roof on this bloody bus shelter? What's the point of a roofless shelter? It's ridiculous! I'm so pissed off that I can barely think straight. Once again, I'm left alone and stranded, trying to figure out what to do with Jaya, and all she can think to say is that she wants to get *married* for crying out loud! What am I going to do? Since she reached adulthood, there just seems to be nothing *out there* for her. All the funding and opportunities of her youth seemed to vanish when she reached eighteen. As I wait for my bus, chuntering furiously under my breath, I masochistically dredge up thoughts of all the frustrated hopes and thwarted plans that have blighted Jaya's adult life so far.

'Hi Izzie,' says a friendly voice. I turn to see Trudi Holt standing beside me. Trudi's daughter, Kerry, has been Jaya's "on-again-off-again" best friend since the day they started college. Trudi and I will never be bosom buddies, but I like her straight-talking, no-nonsense attitude.

'What's up, chick?' she asks, 'missed your bus?'

'No – just had a "progression meeting" with Jaya's tutors.'

'What? You mean they told you to fuck off and fend for yourself?'

I smile mournfully. 'More or less.'

She shrugs. 'I wasn't sure, but I thought this would be their last year.'

'So what's Kerry going to do in September?' I ask.

'*Do?*' repeats Trudi doubtfully, as if the use of such an active verb is overly-optimistic. 'I dunno – stay at home with me, I suppose.'

'Won't she get bored?'

'Well, she hasn't got much choice, has she?' she replies. 'Unless she goes to a day centre for a couple of days a week.'

I barely suppress a snort. 'Kerry wouldn't be eligible for day centre provision – she's like Jaya... not "disabled" enough.'

Trudi nods. 'My eldest... she's proper handicapped. She used to go to a lovely little centre near us, but they closed it down last year.'

'I didn't know you had two daughters,' I say, whilst in my head, an alternative version of my polite comment goes a little something like this: 'You poor cow – how on earth do you cope with *two*?!'

'Yeah, Gemma's twenty-three. She goes to this great big place now... sits around with old people all day. She hates it.'

I nod, sympathetically. That's pretty much my understanding of day centres for the disabled – large, overcrowded and impersonal.

'But what can I do?' she continues, 'when Meadow Park closed, there was nowhere else for her to go. Her social worker said it was better than nothing...'

The look of defeat in her eyes serves only to reignite my burning anger at the unfairness of it all.

'But they can't just close places down without making adequate alternative provision!' I fume, irritated by the posh, whiney quality my voice has taken on. 'I thought the whole point of closing day centres was to replace them with more personalised services!'

'Well, at least it gets her out from under my feet, eh?' she jokes weakly.

But I'm not to be deterred from my soapbox rant. 'I mean, in principal, I agree with a more person-centred approach, but what exactly does that mean in practice?'

She shrugs and sighs. 'I'm buggered if I know, chick.'

'If you ask me, it's all just a conspiracy to slash government spending and pull the wool over our eyes!'

But she's not listening to me anymore. Instead she's focusing on a point in the middle distance.

'Here comes my bus.' She rummages in her handbag and pulls out a crumpled bus-ticket. 'Tell Jaya that Kerry'll see her at Friends For Life tonight.'

I slap my forehead with such ferocity that the poor woman almost jumps out of her skin.

'Jaya!' I screech. 'Oh my God, I've forgotten Jaya!' I cancelled the Ring & Ride when I made the appointment with Mandy. What an idiot!

'Bye Trudi!' I bawl over my shoulder. She watches on in astonishment as I leg it back towards college to find my daughter.

Jaya: Sue won't let me on the Ring & Ride because she says I've been cancelled. Maggie asks who cancelled me and Sue says she doesn't know but that I'm not on her list tonight. I say maybe mum cancelled me because she came to college for a meeting. Where's mum now Jaya? asks Maggie and I say I don't know. Sue and Maggie look at me like they feel sorry for me but I'm not sure why. Then Maggie takes me back into college and buys me a cup of tea.

Izzie: I can see her in the college cafeteria, drinking tea and chatting with a member of staff. As I run towards them, she looks up and smiles in greeting.

'Hi mum, did you forget me?'

The woman she's with doesn't seem quite so pleased to see me. She gives me a curt nod as I breathlessly try to regain my composure.

'So sorry,' I pant.

She turns to Jaya. 'Bye love, see you tomorrow.'

27

'Bye Maggie,' says Jaya brightly.

Maggie leaves and I slide gratefully into the vacated chair.

'Sorry Jay,' I mumble.

She shrugs and continues to smile serenely at me. For some reason, her composure riles me.

'Look, what the bloody hell is going on, Jaya?' I demand.

Her eyes fill with tears and I feel like a total bitch. 'I'm sorry, babe', I say, holding out my hand towards her. 'I didn't mean to shout at you. It's just that I don't understand... why do you want to get married?'

'I just do,' she replies.

'But why?' I ask. 'You don't even have a boyfriend.'

She blushes and I feel a stab of guilt for the way I humiliated her earlier. I try a different approach. 'Don't you want to *do* something with your life?'

She eyes me cautiously. 'Like what?'

'I don't know. Meet new people? Travel? No... maybe that's not such a good idea. How about volunteer work?' She seems to consider the question seriously.

'I'd like to learn to cook...'

'Great! That's a good start.'

'...so I can make nice dinners for my husband.'

My heart sinks. 'Is that really all you want in life? To get married?'

She juts out her chin, defiantly. 'Yes I do, mum!' she says. 'What's wrong with that? Just because you didn't.'

I feel as if she's slapped me in the face. The unspoken accusation hangs heavily in the air between us: we are a one-parent family. She will never have the opportunity to meet her father. I have let her down. I take a wobbly breath.

'That was spiteful and unnecessary, Jaya.'

She looks genuinely surprised. 'Why, mum? I'm only telling the truth. I'm just saying that I don't have to do things the same way as you.'

'I'm not suggesting that you do, Jaya,' I say, coldly.

'What's wrong, mum?'

I sigh and run my fingers through my hair. 'Look,' I begin, taking her hand over the biro-embellished table top, 'I just want what's best for you, Jaya.'

'So, what do you think I should do?' she asks.

'I don't know. I don't have all the answers.' I only wish I *did*. 'It's just... isn't there something *else* you want to do?'

'What else is there, mum?'

I look up sharply and meet her tranquil gaze. There's no trace of anger or hurt in her eyes. In her own calm and logical way, she has reached the very heart of the matter; there *is* no clear path for her towards a productive and fulfilling adult life.

Jaya: Mum seems really gloomy and she's hardly said a word to me since we got back from college. I don't know why she was so angry when I said I want to get married, because I was only telling the truth and mum says I should always tell her the truth, no matter what. I know I haven't told her the whole truth about John and everything but that's because she's being so weird about me having a boyfriend. I'll have to tell her soon because I want her to come to the wedding. Maybe I'll wait until after he's actually proposed. When we get married, she'll see how much we love each other and that'll make it all OK. Then she'll *have* to be happy for me. But I don't think I can wait that long for her to cheer up. I wish she would just cheer up straight away because I don't like it when she's sad. I miss her smiley face. I'm going out in a bit, so I hope she's back to her normal self when I get back.

29

Izzie: As soon as Jaya goes out to her Friends For Life group, I make my way over to Bina's. Kishan answers the door and rocks excitedly back and forth on the spot in greeting.

'Hi mate,' I smile. 'Is your mum in?'

'Mum in... mum in... MUM IN!' he yells, as he runs off upstairs.

I find Bee sitting on the sofa, reading an article in the local paper. She holds it up for me to read the headline.

'Some other poor cow's murdered her disabled kid, then topped herself,' she says cheerily. Her flippancy bugs me.

'I know how she feels,' I say. Bee snorts with laughter.

'Bad day at the office, dear?' I'm treated to a flash of her lovely white teeth.

'It's not bloody funny, Bee!'

'I'm not suggesting that it is,' she says quietly, suddenly serious. I pace her living-room floor.

'I mean, what the hell do they expect us to do? Keep them in a fucking box?!'

'Who are you talking about?'

'Jaya, of course!' I practically yell, 'and Kishan too. Anyone with disabilities over the age of eighteen!'

'Sweetie, calm down. You're not making any sense.'

I try taking a deep breath, but produce instead a demented hiccuping sound.

'Sit down, you silly cow.' She grabs my hand and pulls me down beside her.

'Sorry,' I mutter.

Bina puts a sympathetic arm around me and squeezes me tightly.

'I take it your meeting with Jaya's teachers didn't go so well?'

I shake my head, not trusting myself to answer.

'Do you want to talk about it?' she asks.

30

'Stop being so nice to me,' I mumble into her shoulder. 'I don't deserve it.'

'True,' she replies, 'but someone's got to sort you out when you have a meltdown.'

'Thanks.'

'You're welcome. Now, tell me what happened.'

I take a huge gulp of air. 'They told me her course finishes this year.'

'Oh my life! What does that mean?'

'That she has to leave.' I almost burst into tears at the thought. 'She's so happy there, Bee,' I whimper.

'So there are no other courses at the college?'

'Not for Jaya. She's reached her "academic potential" apparently.'

'Well they might have a point,' reasons Bee.

'Come off it, Bee... it's all bollocks!' I feel my heart rate quicken again. 'Just an excuse to palm her off onto some other service.'

'I'm just saying that if she can't actually achieve the qualification, then—'

'So what now?' I interrupt. 'Depending on who you talk to, she's either not "able" or not "disabled" enough.'

'I know, I know. It's a tricky one.'

'I mean, this is supposed to be a modern, civilised country,' I seethe. 'So why is disability provision so shit?'

Bina shakes her head and laughs. 'That isn't completely true, Iz, and you know it. Look at Kishan. He's happy at the day centre. Where else is he going to go?' She smiles and nudges me gently in the ribs.

'Oxford? Or maybe Harvard?' I giggle in spite of myself.

'OK, so maybe a day centre is the right place for Kishan,' I agree, 'but what about Jaya? What's going to happen to her, Bee?'

31

'Jaya will be just fine,' says Bina, soothingly. 'She has a mother who loves and supports her and this country isn't so bad. Things will get better, you'll see.'

'I know, I know, but that doesn't help me decide what to do about Jaya *now*.'

'Well, have you asked her what she wants to do?'

'She wants to get married,' I murmur, almost inaudibly.

My usually ultra-composed friend is rendered temporarily speechless. 'She wants to... *what*?' she manages eventually.

'Get married,' I repeat.

'Who to?' asks Bee, 'the mystery boyfriend?'

I shrug. 'There isn't one... apparently.'

She looks dubious. 'Are you sure?'

'No,' I reply miserably, 'of course I'm not. I'm not sure of anything any more.'

opportunities

Izzie: A strangulated scream jolts me from my slumber. I leap out of bed, race across the landing and fling open the door to Jaya's room. She is sleeping the angelic sleep of the innocent; her lips parted in beatific smile, her silky hair fanned out across the pillow. I lean against the doorframe, breathless and bewildered. Could it be possible that the awful cry came from me? My pounding headache and damp nightdress suggest that I have not been sleeping so peacefully. I return to my room and get back into bed, but I know there will be no more rest for me tonight. I pull the duvet over my head and await the dawn.

After breakfast, I ring the college and leave Mandy an apologetic answerphone message. I feel bad about the way I spoke to her yesterday. She was only doing her job and none of this is her fault. Before I hang up, I thank her for all the help she and Karen have given Jaya. Feeling in a more positive frame of mind, I put on my coat and leave the house. Within minutes I'm marching to the beat of my pounding heart and, as always, the vigorous exercise eases the pressure in my head. I think about the last time I visited the library. I was looking into starting up my own business. All I had was a name and a vague idea: "Chai-Chai", an Indian-themed café serving wholesome vegetarian food and lashings of free chai tea. I liked the idea of creating little meditation booths out of thick silk drapes where customers could go to relax and take stock before returning to the real world. I look down the deserted high street, its lifeblood drained by the all-consuming Merry Hill Centre. My café would never have worked here, but it's the only time I've ever had a goal that was nothing to do with Jaya.

I log onto a computer and type "employment opportunities, learning difficulties, West Midlands," into Google. I find an employment agency, which caters exclusively for people with learning disabilities. I'm a little dubious. These organisations always seem to crop up out of nowhere and then disappear into thin air. I print off the information anyway and put it in my bag. Back home, I ring up and speak to a hyperactive young kid called Clare. She's nice enough, but seems to be reading from a script. She assures me that Jaya will 'get access to a specialist recruitment advisor who will help her identify her training needs and develop a personalised employability plan'. When I ask her what this will entail, she repeats exactly the same spiel and then adds brightly, 'Is there anything else I can help you with today, madam?' I assure her that there isn't and hope that the "specialist advisor" will have a bit more nous than the telephonist. Clare makes Jaya an appointment for the day after tomorrow and ends the call with an over-zealous 'have a nice da-ay!' It all sounds a bit too airy-fairy for my liking, but the good thing is I've got something positive to tell Jaya.

Jaya: It's really cold outside. I'm waiting for the Ring & Ride to take me home, which I'm very happy about because college was *so* boring today. Karen went on all morning about what we're going to do when we leave this summer and a man did a talk about writing a CV. The man was quite nice actually, but I didn't really listen to him because I already know what I'm going to do when I finish college. My hands are numb. I tell John and he feels them. He keeps his hands on mine until they're nice and warm again. I'm so happy because I'm holding hands with my boyfriend for the second time in two days!

When I get home, I nearly tell mum about John but she wants to talk about me getting a job again. She keeps going on and on about some job interview and then we have a fight. I say I want to get married, but she says I'm a silly little girl. I can't believe she still thinks I'm a little girl! It's so annoying because I'm not and I want to have babies. Why can't she see that I'm not a kid anymore? I could even live on my own if I wanted to. Kerry Holt's cousin lives on her own in sheltered housing. I'm not sure what that means, but I'm going to ask her tomorrow.

Izzie: I'm so anxious to talk to Jaya that I'm hovering by the front door when she comes bounding through it. We collide in the doorway and I have to grip her shoulders to stop myself from falling over. As I stumble into her, she laughs in delight and, in that moment, she has never looked lovelier; the biting wind has whipped crimson into her cheeks and snowflakes dance in her coal black hair.

'Great news, Jay!' I blurt out, keen to add to her good humour. 'I've got you an interview with a job agency.'

I watch as the sparkle leaves her eyes and an all too familiar veil slides down over them; a clever little trick she's perfected over the years which renders their expression unreadable. Whenever she deploys this self-preservation technique, I find myself suddenly staring into the depths of nothingness, trying desperately to uncover meaning beyond the concentric orbs, the golden flecks, the pools of light; a strange sensation, which leaves me reeling and nauseous. It's much the same feeling I used to get as a little girl when I was watching television and the person on television was watching television. I would try to imagine another person on the television on television also watching a person on television (and so on into infinity!) until my head would spin and the concept would become meaningless.

'What's wrong, Jaya? I thought you wanted a job?'

She shakes her head, angrily. 'I already told you what I want.'

'What?' I shout. 'To get married? You need a boyfriend before you can get married, you silly little girl!'

'Well maybe I do have a boyfriend!' she yells back at me.

'Well have you got one, or haven't you?' I make a frantic grab for her hand. 'Just tell me the truth, Jay.'

She jerks her hand away. 'No I bloody don't have a boyfriend!' she bawls, as she stomps off to her room.

As I watch her disappear up the stairs, I experience a moment of intense panic. The thought of her getting married to one of her college or Friends For Life buddies is more than I can cope with at the moment. I mean, where would they live? With *me*? Who would support them, cook for them, help them with shopping and budgeting? And heaven forbid that he should be even less able than Jaya! How would he take care of my little girl then? A shiver goes through me and I feel physically sick. No. She said it herself – there is no boyfriend. She's just got a lot on her plate at the moment. She's probably frightened about the future and having a teenage strop. I need to find a way to take her mind off things. I need to make sure she's got something to do in September.

the interview

Jaya: I can't believe mum's made me come. She woke me up this morning with a cup of tea in one hand and my Topshop suit in the other and said get out of bed Jaya because you're going and that's final. She's such pain. Why can't she just leave me alone? I was really looking forward to a lie-in this morning but instead I'm walking through town with mum in the freezing cold. At least all the Christmas things are out in the shops. I like looking at the decorations in the windows. Maybe mum will take me shopping after. It's the college Christmas disco soon and I need a new party dress.

Izzie: As we walk in, the twitchy receptionist smiles feverishly at us. She stands and holds aloft a typed manuscript before proceeding to read out a polite customer greeting:

'Good morning. My name is Clare. How may I help you today?'

Of course... Clare has a learning difficulty – how stupid of me! I feel instantly guilty as I remember my irritation towards her on the phone. I attempt to make amends now by giving the poor kid a huge smile and warm handshake.

'We've got an appointment with Mike,' I say, 'Jaya Jones.'

'Please take a seat,' she reads, as she wipes off the moisture from my palm onto her skirt.

After a few minutes, Clare shuffles over to us, clutching her manual. 'Mike's ready for you now, Jaya,' she informs me, 'it's just through that door there.'

'I'm actually Jaya's mum,' I say.

'Oh', says Clare. She holds up the script to her face and begins to read frantically to herself.

'It's OK,' I tell her gently, 'you're doing a great job, Clare.' She slowly lowers the papers and smiles timidly at me. She has a beautiful smile.

Jaya: I wish mum had let me come in on my own. I probably won't get a word in as usual. I didn't even get to introduce myself to the receptionist and I'm really good at introducing myself. How do you do? My name is Jaya Jones. Smile. Flick hair. Jaya Jones. I love my name. It's so pretty. I'm glad I haven't got my dad's surname like everyone else because I think Jones goes really well with Jaya. The man is looking at me. I hope he didn't just ask me a question because I wasn't actually listening to him. Maybe mum was listening. I hope so.

Izzie: Why isn't she answering Mike's questions? He's going to think she doesn't understand. I bet she hasn't been listening to him. It's so infuriating! Why can't she take a bit of responsibility, instead of relying on me to do everything for her?

'Jaya, tell Mike what sort of jobs you're interested in.'

She looks relieved, confirming my suspicion that she hasn't been listening.

'I want to work in a clothes shop or behind a make-up counter,' she tells him.

'Uh-huh,' says Mike, 'we have a lot of jobs in retail, so that's good.'

'I don't want to work in retail,' she says huffily, 'I want to work in a shop.'

He smiles at me, in an "ahh-bless" sort of way, which I don't like at all.

'Retail does mean shops, Jaya,' I explain, quickly.

'Oh right. That's good,' she says.

Jaya: Maybe this wasn't such a bad idea after all. If the man can get me a job in a clothes shop or on a make-up counter then that would be really cool. He prints off all the shop jobs for me to look at. It takes me quite a long time to read all the shop names, but when I've finished I don't know why I bothered because they're all supermarkets. Where are the clothes and make-up jobs? I ask him. Well actually we work mostly with big supermarket chains he says. But I don't want to work in a supermarket I say, I want to work in fashion or make-up. Then he winks at mum and says one shop job is pretty much the same as another don't you agree mum? It's a bit of a weird thing to say because she's my mum not his.

Izzie: I'm with Jaya on this one. She's actually pretty knowledgeable about fashion and make-up and I don't like the insincerity of his remark; working in a supermarket is hardly the same as working behind a make-up counter. Still, it would be a good way for her to get some experience in retail and customer service. I turn to Jaya.

'What do you think?' I ask her, 'it might be a good starting point?'

'But mum,' she says, 'you always say that I shouldn't settle for second best and that I should always follow my heart.'

Jaya: Mum goes quiet and the man fills up his cheeks with air and then blows it all out again. Then he says so are there any other jobs you're interested in Jaya? I'm not sure if I should mention looking after babies because mum will probably go mad again. The thing is I really would like to look after babies. I'm good at first aid and I know about sterilising bottles and changing nappies and burping babies after their milk. The student union at college does a parenting taster course and you get to take home a pretend baby for the night. I was thinking of putting my name down for it until mum starting acting all weird about stuff. The man coughs like he wants me to hurry up and it's starting to stress me out so I just say nothing and shake my head. The man sighs but mum smiles at me, so I don't think I've done anything wrong.

Izzie: Well, I can't say I blame her. It's true, I've always told her that she can be whoever she wants to be, so why should she be bulldozed into something she doesn't want to do? I'm actually proud of the way she spoke up for herself, particularly as this bloke has no idea how to communicate with people with learning difficulties.

'Well, if a suitable job comes up, please get in touch,' I say, standing up. He looks mildly surprised.

'Oh, right... OK,' he shrugs.

'Good-bye. Thank you for your help,' says Jaya politely, shaking his hand. She smiles and flicks her hair.

Jaya: As we walk out I say bye to Clare. She smiles and waves at me. She seems really nice. Mum and me go to a café for a drink and a cake. While we're drinking our tea I ask her why she didn't make me take the supermarket job. Because I want you to be happy Jaya, she says. Then mum says I was very proud of the way you handled that. Oh right thanks mum, I say, but why? I don't know, says mum, I suppose I'm just proud of you in general. I'm proud of me too, I say which makes her smile. I ask her what she's smiling at and she says, you know what Jaya you wouldn't have lasted a day in a supermarket. So I ask her what she means and she ruffles my hair and says, you're such a pain in the arse, you'd have probably got the sack by lunchtime. I know she's only joking but it's actually quite a cheeky thing to say.

Izzie: I can't help but laugh at the indignant expression on her face.

'Sorry Jay,' I say, 'I'm only kidding.'

She grunts an unintelligible reply and crams the rest of her iced bun into her mouth. 'I'm eating so I don't have to talk to you,' she says with her mouth full.

'Right... well, telling me that sort of defeats the object of stuffing your face so you don't have to talk to me,' I inform her. She considers this for a moment before sticking out her sugar-coated tongue.

'What a well-brought-up child,' I murmur approvingly, 'please pass on my compliments to your mother.'

'No problem,' she says and, leaning over the table, she swipes some icing off the top of my carrot cake and applies it to the end of my nose. She squeals in delight and we both dissolve into a fit of giggles. I look at her lovely, happy face and think that if I had my way, it would always be adorned with a smile. But this is no time to be whimsical, I chide myself.

'So, where do we go from here, then?' I ask her.

Jaya: We were having such a lovely time but then mum had to go and ruin it all. How should I know where we go from here? I've already tried telling her what I want but it just makes her angry. It's not fair because some of my friends are married and *their* parents didn't try to stop them. Kevin and Jackie met at Friends For Life and they had a big wedding and a lovely honeymoon in Blackpool and everything. I wouldn't want to be married to Kevin but Jackie really loves him so that's OK. Kevin and Jackie even had a baby but they gave it to a man and lady who couldn't have babies of their own. I think they were really nice to do

41

that, but I would never give my baby away. Now Jackie has to have injections so she won't have any more babies. Her social worker takes her for the injections and Jackie says they really hurt but that she doesn't mind because having a baby hurts more. I don't care if it does hurt to have a baby because it would be worth it. When I'm married I'm never going to have injections or take pills. My friend Faisal from college is getting married. His parents have found him a wife from Pakistan and she's coming over to live with Faisal and his family. My mum would never do anything like that for me. Faisal showed me her picture on his phone and she's really pretty and doesn't even mind about his curved spine because she loves him for who he is.

Izzie: Jaya seems to be struggling to come up with ideas, so I make a suggestion.

'I was thinking,' I continue, 'that if we can't find anything in the day, we could look into other social and evening activities... you know, like Friends For Life?'

She perks up at this. 'I love Friends For Life,' she says.

'I know you do,' I reply. 'So how about trying a new hobby? Maybe you could learn to play a musical instrument?'

She shakes her head and gives me the "thumbs down" sign.

'OK, so how about a sport? You could join a netball or a hockey team? Or you could try dance or drama classes?'

'Maybe drama,' she says hesitantly, 'I think I'd quite like that.'

'Great! Actually I've already done a bit of research.' I pull a leaflet out of my handbag and pass it to her. She inspects the picture on the front – a diverse group of smiling individuals in various colourful costumes.

'D-r-a-m-a... F-o-r... A-l-l' she reads.

'It's for people with learning difficulties, just like Friends For Life.'

'OK,' sighs Jaya, 'I'll give it a go.'

drama for all

Jaya: I don't feel like pretending to be a cat. I don't even like cats. They make me sneeze and once one chased me around a park on holiday. No-one believed me after but it actually did chase me and I was really scared. If you don't want to be a cat why don't you pick another animal? says Tracy. Maybe you could be a dog or a rabbit? I don't like dogs or rabbits either I say. Just be whatever you want to be then she says. Everyone else is purring and meowing and licking their pretend paws. Very good says Tracy you're all very good little cats. One lady in a wheelchair hisses at Tracy and Tracy laughs and says brilliant Heather you're an angry cat. Heather laughs and spins round in her wheelchair and accidentally runs over my foot. My foot really hurts so I hop on one leg and Tracy says are you being a bouncy kangaroo Jaya? So I say no Heather ran over my foot and Tracy shakes her head and walks off which is actually quite bad because my foot could be broken. Then Tracy makes us all sit in a circle and we have to pass a smile to each other. The game is that you aren't allowed to smile until someone passes it to you and then you have to put it on your face. It's a really boring game because once you get the smile you don't do anything with it you just put it on your face and then pass it to someone else. I think it would be better if we passed a killer spider around the circle and then we had to pretend to die. I'm really good at pretending to die because I've watched *Eastenders* loads of times so I know exactly what to do. Also I'm really good at first aid because I did a course at school so then I could pretend to be a doctor and bring everyone back to life. I tell Tracy my idea but she says that it sounds a bit hard for some of the others and also a bit frightening. She says that everyone else is enjoying passing the smile but I think they look just as bored as me. I nearly say that to Tracy but I don't because I don't want to be rude and also Tracy is quite scary.

Izzie: 'I don't think Jaya enjoyed it, I'm afraid,' says Tracy. She laughs, a wheezy braying sound, which irritates the hell out of me.

'Oh right.' I turn to Jaya. 'Didn't you?'

'Well, erm...' She trails off and fixes her eyes on a small crack in the wall.

'Why not?' I probe. She shrugs and glances cautiously in Tracy's direction. A harsh, high-pitched rasping noise tells me Tracy finds this amusing.

'Oh please don't worry about offending me, Jaya,' she says, 'just be honest.'

'Well, it was a bit... a bit...' Whatever it was, Jaya can't seem to bring herself to say it.

'I think what Jaya's trying to say *very diplomatically*,' interjects Tracy, 'is that, intellectually, she's too advanced for the level of the group.'

'Does that mean it was boring?' Jaya whispers loudly.

'Yeah,' I sigh. I feel Tracy bristle beside me, but I'm past caring. I turn to her. 'So can't you give her a more challenging role or something?'

'I'm afraid it doesn't work like that,' she snaps. I've clearly offended her artistic sensibilities.

'Well, how exactly does it work, then?'

She exhales dramatically and rubs her temples. 'Look, I'm sorry if you're disappointed, but I have to pitch the session at the level of the majority of the group.'

'That's not a very inclusive approach,' I retort, 'your leaflet says *Drama For All.*'

'Yes, but Jaya is *too* able.'

'What?! That doesn't make sense.' I take a step towards her and she jumps backwards with a yelp.

'I find your aura very intimidating!'

I stare at her in amazement.

'You've got to be kidding me.' But there's no point arguing with the woman; she's clearly unhinged. Jaya's already hovering nervously by the exit, so I turn on my heel and leave.

Jaya: Mum's not listening to me, so I start washing my pretend whiskers and scratching my pretend fleas. She's staring out of the bus window, but in the end she looks at me. What on earth are you doing Jaya? she asks. I'm trying to make you laugh I say. By acting like a dog? she asks. Duh – I'm a cat, can't you tell the difference? I say. Tracy made us all be cats. We had to walk around the room for ages pretending to be cats and I don't even like stupid cats. Mum snorts and begins to laugh and then I start to feel better. Thank God she says because for a second there I thought you'd gone mad. Mad like Tracy I ask and Mum nods and whispers what a flipping mental-case under her breath. Is madness catching then? I ask her. She looks at me with her smiley eyes and says no, but fleas are. Then she starts to scratch her pretend fleas and I do too. We both scratch our necks and arms and tummies so much that the old man sitting behind us moves to another seat.

When we get home mum goes in the kitchen to get dinner ready and I go to my bedroom to do some make-up practice. I bought some new foundation at the weekend and it's a shade lighter than the one I normally buy. I try it with my bronzer and coral lipstick and it looks quite nice but you can tell I'm wearing make-up because my skin is normally much darker. I can't decide whether to wear my new foundation to college tomorrow but I think John will like it because he wrote on Facebook that he likes Cheryl Cole and she always wears loads of make-up *and* fake eyelashes. Maybe I should buy some fake eyelashes like the ones Cheryl Cole wears. Mum would probably tell me off for wasting my money, but if I fluttered them at John, it might make him kiss me. I know he's my boyfriend and everything but I wish he'd just kiss me or ask me out on a date or something. I'll try my new foundation first and if that doesn't make him kiss me then I'm *definitely* buying fake eyelashes next weekend.

insomnia

Jaya: I HATE Kerry Holt! She's the most stupidest cow in the whole of the West Midlands! This morning she told *everyone* at college that I fancy John and it was really horrible. Even Karen found out and she told me off in front of the whole class and said it was just a silly crush. Then she did this embarrassing talk about appropriate behaviour towards staff and personal space at college and everyone kept giggling and staring because they knew it was about me. Now everyone on the Ring & Ride is making fun of me about fancying John, which isn't fair because he *is* my boyfriend, but they're all laughing at me anyway and it's horrible.

When I get in mum wants to know why I'm upset so I tell her Kerry Holt has been really nasty to me and then mum is really nice. She gives me a big hug and we snuggle on the sofa and watch TV. I love my mum so much. After *Neighbours* she asks me why Kerry has been mean to me and I tell her she was probably just jealous because all the boys fancy me, which isn't a lie, because it's true. Then mum asks me again if I've got a boyfriend and I really want to tell her about John, but I'm worried she'll be angry like Karen was, so I say no. Then mum sighs and says I just don't understand this obsession with getting married. So I tell her I want to have a nice house and a husband and babies to love and look after, which is also true.

Izzie: Jaya wants a baby! Of course! My poor darling – she seems so forlorn, as if she's convinced it's just an impossible dream. I can't believe I didn't think of it before. I mean, it's such a basic biological need. At least that explains her sudden desire to get married. Poor Jaya. Oh God, I've really messed up.

Jaya: Mum is crying, but I don't really know why. She just keeps stroking my hair and saying my poor darling, my poor, poor darling and that makes me cry too.

Izzie: My poor darling. She's been asking for my help and I've let her down so badly. I've dismissed her most natural impulse as a fanciful whim. I think I've been struggling to accept that my little girl is all grown up. No – if I'm honest, it's more than that; Jaya's recent preoccupation with marriage has forced me to consider the subject of sex, something that I really don't want to associate with my little girl. Now I'm forced to consider questions that are impossible for me to answer: How much does Jaya *really* know about sex? Is she mentally and emotionally mature enough for an intimate relationship? Would her partner make allowances for her lack of experience and understanding? And... the really big question, the one I ask myself on a daily basis when it comes to Jaya... how far should I get involved? I mean, aren't these issues the very same that we're all faced with as virgins? Doesn't Jaya have the same fundamental right as everyone else to have the same sexual experiences and to make the same mistakes? And who is ever fully mentally and emotionally ready for sex and marriage, anyway? Take me, I'm totally useless when it comes to blokes, so what right have I to stick my nose in my daughter's love life? Then again, can Jaya really be left to make these sorts of decisions on her own? Oh God – it's at times like these that I wish I had a mother to advise me. What do I do? What do I do? *What do I do?*

Jaya: It's really late, but I can't sleep. I hate it when mum's upset and I can't stop thinking about John. He'll make such a great dad. What will our babies look like? Beautiful. My big eyes and his smiley face. I'll love them so much. I can't wait to be a mum.

Izzie: It's really late, but I can't sleep. Two hundred stomach crunches and I'm still not tired. I've resisted the urge to run downstairs and rearrange the kitchen cupboards and I'm now in bed, but there's no way I can calm down until I've decided what to do about Jaya and there's no way I can decide what to do about Jaya until I've calmed down. I've tried everything to help me relax, even meditation, which was once like second to nature to me, but now leaves me feeling fraudulent and faintly ridiculous. So I've now given up on my respective attempts to resolve all my daughter's problems and to reach a trance-like meditative state (admittedly, two rather over-ambitious tasks for one night of insomnia) and have instead resorted to doing what I do whenever I feel overwhelmed, useless, or paralysed with fear and self-loathing; I'm remembering that I was once the kind of girl who thought nothing of grabbing her backpack, passport and dreams and running away to an Ashram in India. The memory, as always, is consoling but, as I lie in my little bed, in my little house, an (almost) middle-aged woman with eighteen years of motherhood and drudgery under my belt, it seems more distant than ever.

I remind myself that, however unlikely it may now seem, that person really was me. Perhaps somewhere deep inside, it still is. I lie back, close my eyes and try to conjure up the girl I once was; how I once looked, how I once felt, what once motivated and impassioned me. My love affair with eastern religion, culminating in my spiritual sabbatical to India, was undoubtedly the driving force of my adolescent life. Although it began as a protest against the sterile, unthinking Christian piety of my parents, my interest in yoga and meditation soon became less about rebellion and more about devotion and worship. In particular, I remember my discovery of Bhakti yoga when I was seventeen as an explosion of love and light in my soul. I loved everything about it; the active participation in worship, the singing, the chanting, the heightened awareness, the sense of connection to a higher being. For the first time in my life I felt a sense of true purpose. From then on, everything else seemed meaningless; college work, friends, boyfriends – all paled into insignificance before my pursuit of spiritual fulfilment. Soon, yoga classes at the local primary school were no longer enough to sustain me spiritually – I yearned for a more authentic experience, a deeper religious understanding. India called!

I would like to be able to boast that my time in the Ashram was the most intense and life-changing of my existence. However, it was the events immediately following my departure from the Ashram which had the more profound and lasting effect on my life. In the Ashram, I learned how to curb my physical appetites, put aside my emotional needs and regard my own ego with the dispassionate air of a stranger. In the nine months after I left the Ashram, my physical, emotional and egocentric selves all resurfaced with a vengeance during a whirlwind succession of sex, conception, pregnancy and childbirth. In the eighteen years since Jaya's birth, India, the Ashram and the girl I once was have all become dim and distant memories and the pressures of being a single parent have taken their toll on me. And so, as dawn breaks over

Netherton, my thoughts return to that most beloved and most agonizing of subjects; Jaya. What do I do about Jaya? The answer comes to me with startling ease. It's simple, really. Love her. Support her. Allow her to grow into the woman she is becoming. Find Jaya a suitable boy.

a suitable boy

Izzie: 'Find Jaya a *what*?!' splutters Bee, almost choking on a mouthful of chocolate fudge cake. She gapes at me, open-mouthed.

'A suitable boy,' I repeat. At the next table, I notice a couple of old dears straining to listen to our conversation. On reflection, perhaps it wasn't such a good idea to mention my plan to Bee in a café at Merry Hill. I should have picked a more appropriate time and place and waited until she was in a better mood. We've had a pleasant enough morning wandering around the shops with Kishan, but Bee's upset because she had an argument with her mother last night. Bee overheard her tell a family friend that there was nothing wrong with Kishan, apart from being "lazy and stupid". As a result, she isn't her usual cheery self this morning and now I feel guilty for dumping my own problems on her.

'Look, don't worry about it,' I tell her. 'Shall we have another coffee?'

'Oh my life!' she exclaims. 'You can't drop a bombshell like that and then change the subject.'

'Well there's not much to talk about. I just want to know if you can help me or not.'

'I don't know what to say,' she replies. 'I mean, have you really thought this through?'

'Of course I have. It's what Jaya wants.'

'But you told me it was just a silly phase.'

'I know.'

'Just a few days ago, you said—'

'I know what I said, Bee!' I interrupt. 'A lot has changed since then.'

'Clearly,' says Bee, raising her eyebrows.

At some point during our conversation, Kishan gets up from his seat, walks over to the old dears' table and helps himself to a buttered scone. Bee and I are so engrossed that we don't notice until one of the ladies lets out a piercing shriek. By this time, Kishan is seated at their table, happily munching on his illicitly acquired scone and helping himself to another.

'What *do* you think you're doing, young man?' asks the sterner-looking of the two women.

'Young man... young man... YOUNG MAN!' repeats Kishan, rocking back and forth.

'Sorry!' says Bee, running over. 'Please let me pay for the cakes my son took.'

'Oh dear,' says the second woman, regaining her composure. 'I didn't realise he was... you know... *special*.'

'Oh yes, he certainly is that,' says Bee, regarding her son's butter-smeared face, fondly. 'Come on mister, you've caused enough trouble for one day.'

She puts a two pound coin on the table and firmly guides Kishan back to his seat. He looks from me to Bee and his face breaks into a huge, devilish grin. Bee catches my eye and we both begin to laugh. It's a welcome distraction in what is turning out to be quite a difficult conversation.

'So, why do you need my help?' asks Bee, picking up from where we left off. 'I mean, wouldn't it be better to let Jaya find her own husband?'

'No,' I say, resolutely. 'I've helped Jaya with every big decision in her life and this is the biggest of all!'

'OK – so how about internet dating? Wouldn't that give her more choice?'

'You must be kidding! That would be just asking for trouble. She's so vulnerable – she'd be bound to meet some weirdo.'

'Like you did, you mean,' she says, darkly.

I hold up my finger, silencing her. 'I don't need to be reminded of that, thank you very much. And anyway, that's exactly why I don't want her going down that route.'

'You're right,' agrees Bee, 'but I still don't think this is the best way—'

'Trust me,' I cut in, 'I've done nothing but think about this for the past week. With an arranged marriage, we both get to choose the bloke. She gets her say and I get mine. It's the perfect compromise.'

Bee looks far from convinced. 'Marriage is a big thing, Izzie and Jaya is… well, without wanting to offend you, she's hardly the most stable and mature of girls, is she?'

'*Please*, Bee,' I plead, 'I've gone over it again and again in my head, doesn't Jaya have as much right as everyone else to marriage and children?'

'Of course! I'm not debating that.'

'She may be a bit vain and fickle at times, but she's serious about this and it's my duty to support and guide her in any way I can.'

Bee exhales deeply and I know she's relenting. I press home my advantage. 'Just put me in touch with a few nice young men, that's all I'm asking. Leave the moral and ethical debate to me.'

'Fine,' she says, eventually. 'I'll introduce you to my dad's sister, Geeta. She knows every Indian family and eligible bachelor in the Black Country.'

'Great! Thanks so much!' I squeeze her hand gratefully across the table. Her eyes lock on mine.

'I just hope you know what you're doing.'

auntie geeta

Jaya: Mum's going to find me a husband! She's gone to meet Bee's auntie, who's going to introduce me to lots of different boys who will all want to marry me. Then I get to pick my favourite one and have a big wedding with a red sari and henna tattoos and *everything*! Of course, I won't actually marry any of them, because I'm getting engaged to John, but it'll be fun to meet some new boys and I might even find someone I like *more* than John. If I do find someone I like more than John, then I'm sure John will understand that I have to have an arranged marriage because I'm Indian. All Indian ladies like me *have* to have arranged marriages, because that's what Indian ladies do and if I don't meet anyone I like more than John, then I can marry John instead!

Izzie: I take an almost instant dislike to Auntie Geeta. I admit I'm initially fooled by her fat, jolly appearance, but I soon realise that her friendly facial expression doesn't extend to her eyes. I'm also mildly put out by her tendency to make catty remarks in a pleasant and jovial manner. Bee treats her with the unwavering respect that many Asian people reserve for the older generations of their family, but I sense from her unusually cagey behaviour that she's no more a fan of Auntie Geeta than I am. We're ushered into Auntie Geeta's garishly decorated living room, where she

57

looks me up and down, as if it is my hand in marriage on offer. She turns to Bee.

'Her daughter is retarded, yes?' She says the word "retarded" with a big feline grin, baring two rows of perfect white teeth.

'I think you'll find, Bua, that is not a politically correct term,' says Bee. She matches her tiger smile, tooth for tooth.

'Shall we say developmentally challenged, dear?' replies her aunt, soothingly, with a placating flutter of her stubby little hands.

'She has a learning difficulty, yes,' I interrupt, 'but with the right support and a suitable boy, she would make a fine wife.' *A fine wife!* Jesus! I'm starting to sound like the old Jewish matchmaker from *Fiddler on the Roof*.

Auntie Geeta nods with fake sympathy. 'A suitable boy?' she says, looking straight into my eyes. 'Indeed, I will be sure to ask all my friends and family if they know of any suitably *challenged* boys.'

As we're walking back to Bee's car, I turn to her in confusion. 'Tell me,' I say, 'because I'm still not sure. Did that go well or not?'

'Sorry sweetie,' she laughs, 'I should have warned you about Geeta – she's a bit of a... a...,' she pauses as she searches for the *mot juste*, '...a bitch,' she says finally. I smile uncertainly and Bee puts a reassuring hand on my shoulder.

'She's also the best damn matchmaker this side of Birmingham. If anyone can find Jaya a suitable boy, Auntie Geeta can!'

Jaya: Indian weddings go on for a long, long time and there are always *millions* of guests. The bride wears lots of jewellery and make-up and has turmeric rubbed into her face to make it glow. I'm looking forward to the big wedding and the jewellery and the make-up, but don't really want the turmeric because it's yellow and yellow doesn't suit my skin tone. Indian brides wear a nose-ring, but mum won't let me have my nose pierced, which is actually a bit unfair because she had hers done when she was seventeen. I'll have to get my nose pierced before the wedding or else I won't be able to wear a nose-ring and I want to do everything properly. Indian brides wear red because it's a lucky colour. Red is a good colour for me, because I've got black hair and brown skin, but if I marry John, I'll have to wear a white dress instead. White suits all types of complexion and hair colour, so I'll look pretty whoever I marry.

Izzie: So, my meeting with Auntie Geeta didn't go quite as well as I'd hoped and now I'm worried that I've bitten off more than I can chew. The problem is, Jaya's so thrilled at the prospect of an arranged marriage, that there's no way I can pull out now. When I get home, she's sitting on her bed, daydreaming. She doesn't even notice me standing in the doorway of her bedroom.

'Penny for them,' I say, smiling. At the sound of my voice, she jumps off the bed and rushes over to me in excitement.

'How did it go? What did she say? Does she know any nice boys? When am I going to meet them?' she asks, breathlessly.

'Whoa – easy tiger!' I laugh. 'It was only a first meeting. We haven't got that far yet.'

'But Bee's auntie said yes?' she asks, her eyes shining with hope.

'Yes,' I reply, 'she said yes.'

Jaya lets out a huge whoop of joy and throws her arms around me. I want to laugh and hug her back, but this isn't the time for frivolity; Jaya needs to know that marriage is a serious business. I peel her arms from around my neck and gently push her away from me.

'Jaya – I'm sure Bee's auntie will do all she can, but it's not certain that she'll find any young men... and if she does, they may not be suitable, or you may not even like any of them.'

Jaya pouts as she processes this information, then she grins at me. 'But I'll have fun looking,' she says.

This time, I can't help but laugh and my laughter bubbles forth from me in a great gurgle of delight. The sound is so spontaneous and unexpected, that Jaya looks at me in surprise.

'Are you happy, mum?' she asks me.

'My darling,' I reply, 'if you're happy, I'm happy.'

narinder

Izzie: We're on our way to our first meeting with a... what should I call him? An eligible bachelor? A suitor? A potential husband? I can't believe how nervous I am! When I got up this morning, my hands were shaking so much, I could hardly hold my toothbrush. As I sit in the passenger seat of Bee's car, I send up a quick prayer of thanks that I have such a supportive and loyal friend; there's no way I could do this alone. I turn to look at Jaya on the back seat; she is positively radiant in her blue and gold sari.

'You OK, babe?' I ask.

'Good thanks, mum.'

Reassured, I sit back in my seat and try to relax by watching the passing scenery from my window. Loyal Black Country lass that I am, I'm struck as always by the raw magnificence of the surrounding local area. I try to picture, as I often do, what Dudley would have looked like five hundred years ago, before we peppered the landscape with factories and chimneys and scarred it with limestone quarries and coal mines. In the distance, I catch a glimpse of Dudley Castle and imagine the medieval ruin as it would have been in its glory days, long before the onset of the Industrial Revolution. I imagine the vast manorial estate which was once Dudley and which included the then obscure and inconsequential village of Birmingham.

'We're here,' says Bina, her voice cutting into my reverie.

She parks up outside a smart detached house in a posh-looking street. My heart skips a beat as I take in the iron gates and the sweeping driveway. I turn to Bina in utter panic.

'Oh God, they're rich!' I whisper.

'So?' she snorts, 'and that is a bad thing, *because...?*'

'What if they don't think we're good enough?'

'Shut-up, you idiot!' she laughs as she gets out the car.

The door is answered by a shy looking young man wearing a smart sherwani and churidar pyjamas. In my stupefied state, I wonder briefly if he's the butler, but then he motions for us to follow him and I notice his twisted hand. I realise that this is Narinder, the young man with cerebral palsy whom we are here to meet. We follow him through to a glamorously decadent living room, which features a dramatic red and blue colour scheme, ornate Indian sculptures and an enormous jewel-encrusted mirror above the fireplace. In the centre of the room is a *huge* crimson sofa with a bright cobalt blue floral motif, which is so dazzling in colour and design that at first I fail to see the tiny, plain-looking woman perched upon it. She seems so out of place in this gloriously opulent room, that when I finally notice her, I can do nothing but gape stupidly. Tongue-tied and rooted to the spot, this is not the first impression I was hoping to create! Luckily Narinder's mother seems oblivious to my embarrassment. She stands gracefully and extends a hand in welcome.

'I am very pleased to meet you,' she says warmly, in beautiful singsong Indian-English, 'please call me Gurpreet.'

She motions for us to sit on the recently vacated sofa and glides towards the door. 'Please make yourselves comfortable,' she says. 'I shall return shortly with refreshments.'

In the absence of his mother, Narinder assumes the role of host and engages us in polite conversation about the weather.

'The weather is unseasonably warm for November,' he remarks.

Bee and I smile, nod and make appropriate murmurs of agreement.

'It snowed last week,' says Jaya.

I look across at her sharply. I can't work out if she's being deliberately disagreeable or just socially awkward.

'You're right,' replies Narinder cheerily, 'I had quite forgotten that cold snap.'

Jaya seems satisfied by this answer and smiles at Narinder. *Socially awkward*, I tell myself, reassured. Gurpreet returns with lemonades and nibbles and the conversation continues to flow easily and pleasantly. I feel myself warming to Narinder; he's charming and well-mannered and is definitely potential son-in-law material. I think Jaya likes him too; maybe it'll be first time lucky!

Jaya: Yuck, yuck, YUCK! I can't believe how ugly he is. He walks with a stick and his toes are turned in, he's got one bent arm and one straight arm and a weird accent, like Mr Kumar in the corner shop near us and I can't even understand a *word* he's saying to me. The worst thing is, mum actually seems to like him! I know she likes him because she's doing that weird smiling and nodding thing she does when she really likes someone. This is the worst day of my life, *ever*!

Izzie: We finish our drinks and it's down to business. Gurpreet turns to her son.

'Narinder, why don't you take Jaya for a walk in the garden?' she suggests.

63

'Yes, indeed. That would be most pleasant,' he replies, as he gets unsteadily to his feet. He offers Jaya his arm, in a touchingly formal gesture and she accepts it, graciously. As soon as they're out of earshot, Gurpreet opens negotiations.

'She's a very pretty girl,' she says. It is a statement of fact rather than a compliment. 'Pale skin. Nice hair. A healthy body.' She lists Jaya's physical attributes as if appraising a prize race horse. I don't take offence and I'm under no illusions; an arranged marriage is above all a business contract. Once Gurpreet is satisfied with the pros, she moves onto the cons.

'I apologise if I seem indelicate, but I would be grateful if you could please explain to me Jaya's mental problem.'

I've been expecting this question and I have my answer already prepared. 'Certainly. Jaya has a mild learning difficulty, which has unfortunately proved difficult to diagnose. When she was a child, her mental capabilities seemed significantly lower than average, but over the past ten years, her speech, understanding and intellectual abilities have greatly improved and she's grown up to be a relatively independent and confident young woman...' I pause to take a breath and meet Bee's gaze as she smiles encouragingly at me from across the vast mounds of blue and red upholstery. 'However,' I continue, 'she's still slow to process new information and is easily confused. She's unable to tell the time and, although she can read and write very basic sentences, she has little grasp of spelling, punctuation and grammar. She can count and do simple addition sums, but struggles with subtraction and, as far as I'm aware, has no other mathematical ability.' I stop, aware that I'm rambling terribly and suddenly afraid that I'm painting a less than attractive picture. 'I'm sorry,' I say, 'is this the kind of information you're after?'

'Yes, yes,' Gurpreet assures me, with a bright and friendly nod, 'I thank you most sincerely for your honesty.'

'She's a good girl,' I add, somewhat lamely, keen to conclude on a positive note.

'Oh yes, she's lovely!' says Gurpreet, with such sincere warmth that I feel instantly better. 'My Narinder is also a good boy,' she says, 'they make a nice couple, don't you think?' She smiles and, in that moment, I know that Jaya has "passed".

Jaya: Thank goodness that's over! I couldn't wait to get out of there. It was so *boring*, which is a shame because I thought it was going to be so much fun. Mum and Narinder's mum ended up talking for ages and ages and we had to go in the garden, which was freezing and Narinder was really annoying because he kept telling me about his stamp collection and I don't care about his stupid stamps because I don't even want to marry him. All I want to do now is watch TV and forget about Narinder and his stamps. I don't even know why people collect stamps, anyway. They all look the same and all have boring pictures on them. John collects *Star Wars* toys, which are much cooler things to collect than boring old stamps. *Star Wars* is a film from the olden days about a man called Dark Vader, who wears a black helmet and breathes really loudly. John told me that he has more than fifty *Star Wars* toys, still in their boxes. So I said that it was a shame they'd never been played with and that he should take them out of their boxes and he laughed. I like it when I make John laugh. I don't think I'll ever meet anyone I like more than John.

Izzie: When we get home, Jaya plonks herself down in front of the television and I make us both a cup of tea. She's been a bit quiet since we left Gurpreet and Narinder, but I suppose she's got a lot to think about. Maybe she's worried about where she and Narinder will live if they do decide to get married. I know it's tradition for the bride to move into the groom's family home, but I'm not sure how Jaya would feel about that. Gurpreet's definitely got the room in that huge house of hers and they'd be far more comfortable than in our cramped old terrace, but we clearly have to discuss the matter in more depth. So, I bring the teas into the living room and settle down beside her on the sofa.

'So Jaya, what did you think of Narinder?' I ask her.

She wrinkles up her nose. 'He walks funny.'

'He has cerebral palsy, Jaya. We talked about it before you met him, remember?'

'And his hand is twisted.'

I sigh and rub my temples. I can't believe how wrongly I've read the situation. 'Is that really all you can think of to say about him?'

She considers the question for a moment. 'He's ugly.'

'Jaya,' I say slowly, 'that's a really shallow and horrible thing to say. Narinder is a lovely young man and he's very pleasant looking. I'm so disappointed in you.'

'But I'm pretty,' she replies.

'*So*?' I say, anger creeping into my voice. The girl is getting far too vain.

'So... I should have a handsome husband.'

I try to remain calm. 'Parents don't match their children on account of their looks. That's not how it works. There are far more important issues to consider.' I look at her intently, trying to figure out how much of what I'm saying she actually understands. 'You're not like other young women. I have to find you a boy who will... appreciate your particular qualities. Do you understand what I'm saying?'

She looks at me thoughtfully and seems to carefully evaluate my argument.

"He's yuck!" She sticks two fingers into her mouth and makes a retching sound.

aniij

Izzie: Aniij Sharma. Contender number two. He flashes me a Bollywood smile and compliments me on my dress.

'You have a very beautiful mother, Jaya,' he says.

Jaya utters a suitably simpering response and targets him with her huge moon eyes. She seems totally smitten, but then what do I know? I was wrong last time and this time I'm reserving judgement. As for me, I'm not at all convinced I like him. I've never been comfortable with this type of obsequious flattery and Aniij's warm words of welcome leave me cold. What's worrying me more though, is that I can't work out what's "wrong" with him. I feel terrible for thinking like this. The two things that really make my blood boil are disability discrimination and prejudice but, in this bizarre and ironic twist of fate, I've judged Aniij unfavourably because he *doesn't* have a disability. I'm also slightly troubled by the realisation that I would rather see Jaya married to someone with some form of disability. I mean, who's to say that a disabled person would make a better match for Jaya than someone without a disability? Are disabled people kinder? More accepting? Do they make better companions? Again I realise I'm guilty of the most ridiculous prejudice. It was Auntie Geeta, of all people, who pointed this out to me.

'As far as I know, he doesn't have a disability,' she told me.

I was immediately suspicious. 'Why does he want to meet Jaya, then?'

'I suppose his parents have heard she's a pretty girl,' she replied. Her beady little eyes scrutinised mine with startling intensity. 'Tell me Isabel,' she said, 'is a disability a prerequisite for all Jaya's suitors?'

'No, of course not!' I did a good job of sounding indignant, but I knew in my heart that I wasn't being honest with her.

Aniij darts another dazzling grin in my direction. 'It's easy to see where Jaya gets her good looks from.'

Aniij Sharma is a charmer all right. I say this to his parents and they find it hilarious. 'I'm sorry, did I say something funny?' I ask.

Mr Sharma is unable to reply as he's still rocked by incomprehensible mirth and for some odd reason, Jaya's laughing too. Mrs Sharma covers her mouth with her hand and smothers another giggle.

'I'm sorry,' she says, 'it's just that Aniij means "charming" in Hindi.'

Jaya: Aniij is fit! He's so much nicer than ugly old Narinder and he's got even bigger arm muscles than John. I can tell he really likes me because he keeps looking at me and smiling and it makes me feel all tingly, just like it does when John looks at me. While mum is chatting to his parents, he bends down in front of me and pretends to tie his shoelace. Then he looks me up and down and says, man you are one hot babe, but he says it really quietly so my mum and his mum and dad can't hear. He sticks his tongue out and licks his lips in a sexy way, which is really funny. I start laughing and Mr and Mrs Sharma start laughing too, but I'm not sure why because Aniij has his back to them.

Everyone's laughing apart from mum and she looks quite upset, so then I feel sorry for her and I stop laughing. Then everyone else stops laughing and my mum and his mum start talking and it's all really boring. Then Aniij asks me if I'd like a guided tour of the house and I say yes please, but his dad says no Aniij, I don't think that's a good idea. Aniij gets angry and says a really bad swear word to his dad. He bangs the coffee table with his fist and starts shouting at his dad and his dad and mum look really frightened and I'm frightened too. Then Aniij grabs his dad by the throat and his mum starts to scream and says please no, Aniij. Then she tries to get Aniij off his dad and my mum helps her and she manages to pull Aniij's hands from around Mr Sharma's throat, which is the bravest thing I've ever seen my mum do. Aniij runs out of the room and I hear the front door slam and his dad falls to the floor and I'm really scared because I think he's dead. Then he starts coughing, which is good because it means he's not dead and Mrs Sharma bursts into tears. She sits down on the floor next to her husband and puts her arms around him and mum says shall I call an ambulance? Mrs Sharma says please don't and please never mention this to anyone and please leave, so we do.

Izzie: I now know what's wrong with Aniij. He's a fucking psychopath!

naveen

Izzie: He sits in the corner, mute and immobile. We sip cloudy water from tall glasses and steal nervous glances in his direction.

'So, Naveen, do you like music?' I ask him. It's not a good question, but it's the first thing that comes into my head. Naveen's face remains blank and expressionless and I decide that enough is enough. His mother re-enters the room carrying a plate of samosas.

'Thanks, but I'm afraid we won't be staying,' I say as politely as I can.

Placing the samosas in front of me, she continues to fuss around me as if I haven't spoken. I try again. 'I'm sorry, but—'

She glowers at me, imposing and impervious. 'Eat!' she commands.

Jaya: She's the rudest lady I've ever met and I don't know why mum doesn't just tell her to get lost. She keeps pointing at the horrible samosas but I don't want one. They look gross, all greasy and slimy and they smell disgusting. The boy in the corner is really creepy. He doesn't move or talk and just stares at the wall with a weird look on his face. It's freaking me out because I think maybe he's a zombie or a shop dummy or something. I saw a film once about a shop dummy that came alive at night and it was really scary. Mum tells me I shouldn't watch scary films, but I'm old enough to watch whatever I want. Mum's just taken another samosa which is really annoying because that means we'll have to stay a bit longer and I want to go home. I wish I'd never said I want to get married now. If I hadn't said anything then mum wouldn't be making me meet all these horrible boys and their weirdo families. I don't want to do it anymore. I don't want to meet any more boys. I already have a boyfriend and he's not ugly or mad or dumb, so I'd rather marry him instead.

Izzie: The samosas are actually pretty good and it would be rude to sit here, eating her food without at least trying to make conversation.

'How old are you, Naveen?' I ask him. Silence. I turn to his mother. 'How old is Naveen?' I ask her.

In response, she motions towards the samosas and imitates eating.

'Yes – they're very good,' I tell her, 'I've already had two.' She nods towards Jaya, raising her thin eyebrows.

'Not hungry,' mumbles Jaya, tugging on her coat. Taking her cue, I pick up my handbag and umbrella and offer our hostess an apologetic smile.

'We really do need to go now,' I say. 'Thank you for the food, it was lovely.'

'She clean?' asks Naveen's mother.

I drop my handbag in confusion. 'I'm sorry, but are you asking if my daughter is... clean?'

She clicks her tongue in frustration and, picking up an imaginary duster, mimes wiping the table.

'Clean? Clean?' she asks me.

Jaya tugs at my sleeve. 'Mum, please can we go?' she whispers. There are tears in her eyes.

'Yes babe,' I reply. I stand and Jaya takes my lead. Oblivious to our discomfort, Naveen's mother is now pushing an invisible mop around the floor. Satisfied that I now understand, she fixes me with a fiercely interrogative glare.

'Clean?' she repeats.

Jaya: Thank God that's over. I wish the bus would go faster because I'm tired and wet and I just want to get home. Mum's looking at me like she does when she wants to have a proper good chat but I'm worried in case she wants to talk about meeting more boys. Jaya? she says like she does when she wants to ask me a serious question, so before she can say anything else I jump in really quickly and say please mum I don't want to meet any more boys. Mum goes quiet then she laughs and says thank goodness for that because neither do I. Phew that was easy. Now I just need to work out how to tell her about John. First though I need to see him. Just the two of us on our own. I have to tell him how much I love him because I've never told him before and he needs to know. Then we can be together properly and start to plan our wedding. I think I'll write him a letter and ask him to meet me after college. I hope he proposes straight away. That'll make mum happy too because then she won't have to worry any more about finding me a husband.

Izzie: Bee's on her way over to try out a new dress design on me. She's so talented and normally I love being her model. This evening, though, I feel overcome with fatigue and the house is a mess. I've spent so much time on this ridiculous failed husband-finding mission that I've let everything else around me go to pot. As I half-heartedly push the vacuum around the living room, I'm reminded of the woman and her invisible mop and give up half way through. Bee will just have to take me as she finds me. I flop down on the sofa.

'Jaya?' I call. Our terrace house is so tiny that I know she can hear me from upstairs. She doesn't reply, which tells me she's still moping about her bedroom. She's barely said two words to me since we got home. I know she's annoyed that it didn't work out, but I wish she wouldn't treat me like the bad guy. Well, for once, I'm not going to tiptoe upstairs, knock discreetly on her door and diplomatically restore the peace. Just for tonight, I'm going to try to forget about Jaya's problems. Anyway, it's about time I started sorting out my own shitty life. Maybe it's a good thing Bee's coming over after all. It'll do me good to see a friendly face.

Jaya: Writing is hard. You have to remember lots of things like capital letters and full stops and spellings. I know how to spell lots of words but sometimes I get muddled up. What really confuses me is words which sound the same but which mean different things and are spelt differently. I also get mixed-up over words which are spelt the same but mean different things. The thing is when I try to remember all the different rules then the words I actually want to write go out of my head. I'm trying really hard to spell everything right and I'm breaking each word down like mum taught me. John knows I need help with my writing so I hope he won't mind about the spellings and stuff. I hope he won't think I'm thick.

Izzie: The persistent knocking permeates my slumber and forces me to open my eyes. I must have dozed off on the sofa. I was dreaming that Bee and I had our own little café, selling samosas and saris. It was brilliant. I rush to open the door to my cold and grumpy friend.

'I've been knocking solidly for ten whole minutes!'

'Sorry,' I grin sheepishly, 'fell asleep.'

'I know! I could see you through the window, out cold on the blinking sofa!'

'Sorry,' I repeat. 'Cup of tea?'

'Oh my life,' she grumbles, 'is that really the best you can do?'

'How about a little nip of whiskey?'

'Now you're talking,' she grins, 'make mine a double!'

I waggle my finger at her. 'You're a bad influence on me, Bina Patel!'

Jaya: *Dear Jon i no you luv me and i hop you no i luv you to. The other week wen you held my hand in class and sed it wos our secret it made me very hapy. Then wen we wos waitin four the ring n ride you held my hand again i wos so hapy you wos my boyfrend. i luv it wen you call me sweethart and wen you put your arm arownd me. i no you are staff but it dos not mater. we are neerly the same age and no one can stop us been together. Meet me bye the bus stop outsid college tomorow. i luv you fourever. jaya xxx*

Izzie: Bee is kneeling at my feet, preoccupied by the hemline of her latest creation. She's unusually quiet and I know she's missing Kishan.

'Did he get off OK?' I ask.

'Fine,' she mumbles, her mouth full of pins.

'No tantrums this time?'

She shakes her head. 'He likes the place. He'd just rather be with me.'

I nod. 'Of course he would, but you deserve the odd weekend off, Bee.'

'I know,' she sighs, 'and the respite carers are great.' She gets to her feet and smiles at me. 'They had a *Carry On* DVD waiting for him in the Day Room.' We laugh and she returns her attention to the dress. I watch her nimble fingers darting back and forth, deftly pleating and pinning as the intricate design takes shape. She works in silence, absorbed by her work and I allow myself to be lulled by her rhythmic breathing and calm industriousness.

'So how's the man-hunt going?' she asks suddenly, breaking the spell she has unintentionally woven around me.

I don't really want to talk about it, but I owe her an update. 'It's not,' I reply.

'Really? I thought you met one today.'

'We did, but it didn't go so well.'

'Oh?' She raises an eyebrow quizzically, but doesn't look up.

'He didn't speak,' I tell her.

'The strong, silent type?' she asks, hopefully.

'More like the silent silent type,' I reply.

'So what happened?' she asks.

'Not much. It was more like a job interview.' I squeal as she inadvertently jabs me in the hip.

'Sorry, hon,' she says absently, 'go on.'

'Nothing to tell, really,' I continue. 'His mum didn't speak much English and he didn't speak at all, so we left.'

'Sounds awful,' says Bee, 'so you're giving up on the whole thing?'

'I think Jaya's had enough,' I say. 'Could you let Auntie Geeta know?'

'Of course.' She takes my hand and twirls me gently, admiring her handy-work. 'You should be a model, Iz,' she says.

'Yeah?' I look down at the first phase of my new dress, expertly tacked to follow and enhance the lines of my body. 'And you should be a famous fashion designer, but life's a bitch.'

She laughs and looks away, coyly. 'Actually, I've taken your advice and started to look into local craft fairs.'

'Really? That's great news, Bee!' Forgetting the pins, I go to give her a hug and she gives me a good-natured shove.

'Oi, watch it,' she says.

'Sorry,' I laugh, 'I'm just really pleased.' I motion to my beautiful dress, which just an hour before had been an ordinary piece of material. 'You'll make a bomb.'

'I doubt it, but I'll never know unless I try.' I squeeze her hand.

'I'm proud of you,' I tell her.

'I'm sorry the whole matchmaking thing didn't work out,' she says. 'You OK about it?'

'To be honest, it's probably for the best,' I say, 'and hopefully it's put Jaya off men for life.'

She laughs softly. 'In your dreams, sweetie. In your dreams.'

PART TWO
JOHN & RICHARD

'Rarely are sons similar to their fathers.'

Homer

father and son

John: It's been a long day and the last thing I need right now is yet another of dad's interminable lectures. Unfortunately, dad and I seem to disagree on this point, as we do on most other subjects; he clearly thinks that his pedantic, disapproving little monologues will eventually have some sort of improving effect upon his wayward son, where as I am personally of the opinion that they are the inane ramblings of a patronising old bastard.

John, you total cock! That's way too harsh. Be nice. If only he would shut up for just one second so I can think a nice thought about him. Come on John, you know he only wants what's best for you. There! A nice thought. I can think more clearly now. What's he actually saying?

'...so what do you think?'

I look at my father blankly.

'About what?'

'For God's sake, John – have you been listening to a word I've been saying?'

I take a wild stab in the dark. 'You want me to give up being a teaching assistant?'

'Of course I want you to give up being a teaching assistant – goes without saying – bloody ridiculous job! Now, what do think about this accountancy position in London?'

79

I breathe out slowly. When is he going to get it into his head that I'm never going to be some hot-shot accountant, or banker, or lawyer?

Why don't you just try being honest with him? Tell him how you feel. You never know, he might actually understand!

'Dad, please try to understand. I'm not trying to annoy you in any way by my choice of career.' I pause to smile reassuringly at him, but he rolls his eyes.

Don't give up, John!

'Getting this job is the best thing that's ever happened to me,' I continue, 'I love my work, I love helping people and I love that I'm making a *difference*, you know what I mean?'

Dad makes a sound half way between a snort and a laugh and I can't work out if he's choking or openly mocking me.

'What utter, *utter* crap!' he barks.

Richard: I can tell John's not interested, but I'm determined to have my say for once. It's not often I insist on being listened to, but I just can't sit by and watch him throw his life away. So I try to ignore the infuriating "there's-nothing-in-this-world-you-could-possibly-say-of-interest-to-me" look in his eyes and plough on.

'It would be the perfect opportunity for you. You'd be able to put your Economics degree to good use – processing accounts transactions, analysing statistical data, book keeping – that sort of thing – and you'd also get a good working knowledge of UK taxes and VAT regulations. Sounds fantastic, eh?' No response. I must be a total masochist, but still I persevere. 'The really great thing is...' I pause for dramatic effect – this should make him sit up and listen, '...Bruce is willing to take you on *without* you having to go through the formal application procedure.

He'd be doing it as a favour to me, of course, but I've assured him you've got what it takes to be a top accountant!'

Not even a glimmer of interest. Bloody wonderful! I've spent a whole month buttering up that cretin Bruce Johnson – even promised him an all-expenses-paid week at the villa this summer – all for nothing. One last try.

'So what do you think?'

He looks at me blankly. 'About what?'

The ungrateful, inconsiderate little idiot! I stare at him, with his self-consciously windswept hairstyle and his infantile *Star Wars* T Shirt. He's got such a lot of growing up to do. He's always been childishly obstinate, but this ridiculous act of rebellion is going to end up costing him his career. Well, I've done everything within my power to help him. Now he's on his own. If he wants to waste the rest of his life pushing wheelchairs and wiping arses, then it's no skin off my nose!

John: I'm so depressed after my "cosy" little chat with dad, that I head straight for my bedroom, chuck myself on the bed and call Sarah. She answers almost immediately.

'Hey, handsome.'

I find it an incredible turn-on that, even after a year together, the sound of her voice still makes my heart beat that little bit faster.

'Hey, beautiful.'

'You OK?' she asks. 'You sound a bit down in the dumps.'

'I just miss you, that's all.'

Liar! Tell her the truth, John.

'Oh and also, my dad thinks – and I quote – that my job is "bloody ridiculous" and that I should move to London to work for his wanker mate, Bruce.'

She considers this for a moment. 'Well, you'd be closer to me.'

'Sarah!' I explode, 'my dad is trying to take over my life by bullying me into some crappy corporate job I don't want!'

'I was joking,' she says in a small voice.

'I've already wasted three years at uni doing a pointless degree that *he* insisted I do and I'm fucked if I'm going to —'

'Hey!' she interrupts in a firmer tone. 'I said I was joking, OK? Lighten up!'

Nice one, John. Very smooth!

'Sorry, babe. I didn't mean to snap. He just really wound me up.'

She's not so easily placated. 'And what do you mean you "wasted" three years at uni?' she says huffily. 'You met me, didn't you?'

'I ay havin' a go at yow, wench,' I say in the broad Black Country accent that always creases her up, 'yow'm bloody great, yow am!'

'You prat,' she giggles.

Phew! Good recovery, John old son.

'So, apart from falling out with your dad, how was your day?' she asks.

'Good,' I reply. 'I'm loving my new job. It's knackering, but loads of fun.'

'You're lucky,' she sighs, 'I wish I could say that about my job.'

'It's your own fault for being so brainy – and boring.'

'What's that supposed to mean!?'

'Well, you've done well to get such a good graduate job, but it was never going to be a barrel of laughs at I.P. Freely, was it?'

She laughs out loud at this. 'J.P. Morgan, you dickhead!'

Her good mood restored, we say our usual soppy goodbyes and hang up. I lie back on the bed feeling far happier and more relaxed than I did earlier. I roll over to grab the remote control on my bedside cabinet and, as my backside moves across the bed, I feel the crunch and rustle of paper in the back pocket of my jeans. I slip a hand into my pocket and pull out an envelope with my misspelt name scrawled across the front in spidery felt-tip.

What the...?

Then I remember. Jaya passed me a note at lunchtime today. I'd assumed it was from her mum, but I was on my way to the loo to help a lad in a wheelchair, so I'd stuffed it into the back of my jeans without thinking. As I rip open the envelope, I wonder vaguely why Jaya would be writing to me. I settle back against the pillow and begin to read.

the letter

John: Karen puts down the letter, drums her fingers on the desk and peers at me from over the top of her glasses.

'This is very serious, John,' she says.

'Yeah,' I agree, 'that's why I thought it best to show it to you. What do you think I should do?'

She fills her cheeks with air and lets them deflate slowly. 'Well, first of all we need to interview Jaya to find out what she has to say. Her mother will have to be called in, of course.'

What?! Surely that's not necessary!

'Really?' I ask, as nonchalantly as I can. 'Can't we sort it out between us? Give Jaya a firm talking-to or something?'

Karen looks at me as if I'm the biggest moron on the planet.

'John, I don't think you quite appreciate the gravity of the situation. These are very serious allegations. According to Jaya, the two of you are having some sort of romantic relationship.'

Oh, shit! Why the hell did you show her the letter, John? You total twat! Now she thinks you're some kind of sex fiend!

'But it's not true. She's made it all up!'

'Of course,' says Karen, 'but I'm afraid your word isn't quite enough in this instance. I'll need to be able to categorically prove that there's been no hint of professional misconduct – the Senior Management Team will demand that at the very least.'

The Senior Management Team?! Oh fuck!

'The Senior Management Team?'

Karen smiles, humourlessly. Why have I never noticed before what cruel, hard little eyes she has?

'Don't look so worried, John. I'm sure you'll be found to be totally blameless. It's just...' she pauses and makes an irritating clicking sound with her tongue, '...I do seem to recall an incident in an ICT class when you had your hand on Jaya's...'

The bitch!

'I was *helping* her,' I say. To my dismay, I can't quite keep a note of fear from creeping into my voice. 'She was struggling to control the mouse and she asked for my help. I was just doing my job.'

'Still, you must be aware that as a college we strongly discourage any sort of physical contact between staff and students. It was an integral part of your induction training, if you remember.'

'Of course,' I reply.

'Good,' she says, 'so can you assure me that you have never...,' she refers back to the letter, '...put your arm around her, called her "sweetheart", or held her hand at the bus stop?'

I hesitate before answering, whilst internally my conscience does battle with my sense of self-preservation.

'Because,' continues Karen, 'I'm sure you can see how such actions might easily be misconstrued by a young woman as vulnerable and impressionable as Jaya?' She raises her eyebrows, quizzically and I manage a nod. 'It would also be seen by the college as extremely unprofessional behaviour on your behalf and would no doubt require further internal investigation.'

Lie, John, lie!

I swallow hard and force myself to look Karen in the eye. 'I swear to you that I have no idea what Jaya is going on about.'

'Jolly good,' says Karen briskly. 'Well you've got nothing to worry about then, have you?'

Richard: At first I'm not sure I've heard him correctly.

'Sorry son, come again?'

John looks around the room, as if wanting to make sure that there are no other witnesses to his shameful admission.

'I need your help, dad.'

Blimey! The last time I heard John say those words he was seven years old and learning to ride his bike. Even then, the stubborn bugger waited two weeks before he came to me. I'd been looking forward to teaching him to ride that bloody bike, too – a bit of father-son bonding. Shame John didn't see it that way. Every day he'd sneak the damned thing out onto the driveway and spend hours wobbling and crashing around on the tarmac in front of the house. He only asked for my help in the end when he was so bloodied and battered that he looked like he'd had a double knee and elbow amputation. But that's John for you – as pig-headed as they come!

'What's the problem, son?'

He hesitates and seems to be having second thoughts, but eventually blurts it out. 'I've got myself into a bit of trouble and I need your advice.'

I don't like the sound of this. 'You've knocked up your young lady friend?' I ask, fearing the worst.

'Dad!' he exclaims. 'Do you think I'm stupid, or what?!'

'Well what the bloody hell is it then?'

The words come out a little harsher than I'd meant them to, but the lad's got me worried.

'Forget it!' he yells. 'I'll deal with it myself.'

He flounces off like a prepubescent girl. For all my tact and delicacy, I sometimes find that conversing with my son requires levels of skill and diplomacy which are beyond even me!

John: I should have known dad would be totally useless! When has he ever been there for me? What the hell am I going to do now?

Think John, think! Is there anyone else you can go to? Mum? No, she'd totally freak out. Sarah? Don't be a twat! Do you want her to dump you? Well, old son – it looks like you're on your own. Now just chill out and think things through calmly.

OK – maybe things aren't quite as bad as they seem. I haven't actually done anything wrong. Karen will speak to Jaya and she'll realise that it's just a silly schoolgirl crush. At worst, Jaya will say that I rubbed her hands when they were cold and occasionally call her 'sweetheart'. That hardly makes me Jack-the-fucking-Ripper, does it?!

date night

Richard: Alice is out with the girls and John's gone into Birmingham with his workmates, so the house is empty and quiet. I'm glad. I don't think I could do this if they were here. I don't feel guilty exactly. It's just that, at this precise moment, I don't particularly want to be reminded that I'm a husband and father. I'm ready, but it's still too early for me to leave, so I pad around the house in my socks, drinking beer and steeling myself.

I end up in my bedroom – our bedroom, and find myself sitting at her dressing table. It's strange, I've lived in this house for over twenty years and I've never sat on this seat. I swivel on the pink floral stool, a hideous piece of furniture, and gaze around the bedroom. This is the first time I've ever seen it from this angle. The familiar walls, furniture and belongings seem somehow alien and different. It makes me feel like a stranger in my own home. I turn back towards the dressing table and study her knick-knacks, all her pretty, useless things. Pretty and useless. A perfect description of Alice. This makes me smile and, having mentally belittled and minimised my wife, I am able to flick her off my conscience like a bothersome piece of lint and to continue with the task ahead.

The laptop is still on the bed where I left it. I flip it open and type in the web address. Her profile is the only one in the "my favourites" section of the site. Jayde. No surname. It probably isn't even her real name. Personally, I preferred a famous pseudonym. T.J. Hooker. Veteran police officer. Hard as nails. At the time I felt it was an accurate enough projection of who I am. It would let women know that I'm no spring chicken, but that I'm as strong and virile as they come. But now I wonder if this is really who I am? Is this how people still see me? Is this how I see myself? I shake myself back into the present. Now isn't the time for a fucking identity crisis. I open her last email:

Hi Richard, or should I say TJ? LOL :-)

Looking forward to finally meeting you on Friday. Drinks at The Plough sounds fine. We could maybe go on from there if all goes well ;-)

Love J x

Go on from there? A winking emoticon! Sounds promising. But does she mean...? No point speculating, I suppose. I'll know soon enough. The thought of having carnal knowledge of a woman who is not my wife sends a shiver down my spine which is not altogether pleasant. I take another look at her photograph. A self-conscious mug shot of a heavily made-up face resting on a tastelessly bejewelled hand. She is the sort of woman my mother would describe as brazen. She has unashamedly fake hair, nails and skin tone. Not my type at all, but beggars can't be choosers. She seems interested in me and I'm therefore pathetically grateful. Another man might feel miserable and depressed by this whole, desperate situation, but self-pity has never sat well with me. Far too self-indulgent. I slam my laptop shut. It's time to go.

John: On a scale of one to ten, this night out barely scrapes a two. For starters, I'm not a fan of work "dos". I just don't see the point of going out drinking with your workmates – it's a recipe for disaster! At work you have a professional persona; a smarter, smoother, more polished version of yourself and this is clearly how you would like your colleagues to perceive you. Why then would you want those very same colleagues to witness you making a drunken twat of yourself on the dance floor? Besides, I don't trust some of these so-called "professionals" as far as I could throw them and the last thing I want is a video of me doing the Macarena with my pants down popping up on YouTube. So I'm keeping my arse firmly planted on this barstool and as far away from the dance floor as possible. Unfortunately, Karen's hardly left my side all evening and I'm ninety-nine per cent sure that she's been flirting with me, which is another reason why I'm not having the best of nights. Apart from the fact that I'm not in the slightest bit attracted to her, there's something about the way she's been looking at me that makes me feel uncomfortable. She's just nipped to the loo, so maybe I should slip away quietly now.

Richard: What a dump! Hardly my scene, but then I suppose you have to make certain allowances when you're out with a woman half your age. At least there's no chance of bumping into anyone I know here and Jayde seems to be enjoying herself. She seems OK, actually. She's wearing less make-up than she was in the picture and she's dressed far more demurely. The conversation has been flowing relatively easily, despite the lack of common ground and interests, and largely due to the copious amounts of alcohol we've both consumed. On the whole though, it hasn't been a bad evening and, if I'm not much mistaken, things now seem to be hotting up between us! As I wait to be served, she gyrates against me in time to the music.

'Dance with me, Richie.'

Richie? Nobody calls me that! Under normal circumstances I'd have a stern word, but this is the first time my cock's been hard in months and it's making speech rather difficult. Instead I take hold of her and kiss her hard on the lips.

'Come with me, now!' I urge. 'Let's get a hotel room.'

She pulls away from me. 'Look, Richie... you're well sexy, but let's take things slow,' she purrs.

'Let's not,' I whisper in her ear, my hand creeping up the inside of her blouse.

'Richie!' she giggles, 'I'm not that type of girl.'

Flirting. I think I remember how to do it. 'Oh, really? I was under the impression that you were.'

I manage to seize her wrist before her hand makes contact with my face. Copper's reflexes.

'You bastard!' she hisses. 'Are you calling me a slag?'

'I'm sorry if I offended you – I thought we were...'

But she's already gone. I turn back to the bar and order a triple whiskey.

John: Too late! Karen's coming back over and she looks wasted. What the hell happened to her? I thought she was only going for a pee!

'Not leaving already are we?' She's so close to me that her gin-laced saliva spatters against my cheek and I can clearly see the tell-tale traces of white powder around her hairy nostril. I recoil from her in disgust.

'Well, yeah. I am, actually. Night.'

I smile politely and make to leave, but she bars my way. She smiles, presses herself against me and glues her moist, fleshy lips to my ear.

'Tell you what,' she whispers, 'you come back to mine tonight and I'll personally see to it that a certain letter from a certain student finds its way into the paper shredder. What do you say?'

What do I say? I say that my cock has shrivelled to the size of a peanut at the mere thought of it. I say that I'd rather slap my balls against a cactus. I say that, given the choice, I'd prefer to sleep with a sex-starved female orang-utan... on a bed of nails! I say...

'Well that's a very tempting offer, Karen.'

Her eyes narrow. 'But...?'

'But, I have a girlfriend.'

'Who? Jaya?'

'What?! No! Of course not! Her name is Sarah. Why would you say that?'

Her cruel sneer fills me with alarm, but she manages a good imitation of a laugh. 'Relax, John. I'm kidding.'

She sways in time to the music and then suddenly, with startlingly agility, she begins to shimmy up and down the length of my body. My first instinct is to quickly scan the bar area to make sure no-one's watching, or worse still, capturing the moment for posterity. Unfortunately, the slight delay in the speed of my rebuff is all the encouragement Karen needs and within seconds she's dry-humping my leg. I take her firmly by the shoulders and hold her at arm's length.

'Karen, I'm flattered. Really I am, but I'm in a serious relationship and care very deeply about my—'

'OhshutthefuckupyouspinelesspieceofSHIT!' The sheer force and unexpectedness of her fury knocks the breath out of me. For a few seconds I can do nothing but stare. Then I turn my back on her and make my way towards the exit.

Adrenalin pumps through me as I jog down the steps. I can't believe what just happened in there. I start to feel light-headed and I'm forced to sit down on the ground outside the nightclub.

'Yow alroit, cock?'

The bouncer in front of me is absolutely *huge*. There's a lot of blokes like him in Dudley. The source of their gene-pool is a deep, dark Black Country pit and their strength is born from hard graft. After all, only the very fittest of the fittest families would have survived generations of back-breaking labour and polluted air.

'I'm not pissed, mate,' I tell him, yet still he eyes me suspiciously. To prove my sobriety, I stand up and walk in a fairly accurate straight line. Appeased, he lumbers off. I could really do with a fag right now. I look around for someone to bum a cigarette off and spot an old bloke coming out of the club and lighting up. As he takes his first drag, he closes his eyes and teeters precariously at the top of the steps. Sad really, going clubbing and getting plastered at his age. I wave to get the poor old pisshead's attention.

'Excuse me, mate...' He looks down at me and squints to focus his eyes. 'Got a spare... DAD?!'

Richard: JOHN?! It's John! What the hell is he doing here? I thought he was out in Birmingham. What do I bloody tell him? Maybe I can convince him I'm undercover...? No, he'll never fall for that. Oh shit, I am so drunk and I've got a cigarette in my mouth! *Quick*, get rid of the cigarette. Good... I don't think he saw it. Right, now... compose yourself, Richard.

John: I watch in horror as dad falls head first down the steps and lands at my feet. Blood trickles down his forehead and he emits a low moaning sound. Shit, shit, SHIT! This could be serious! I try frantically to remember what I learnt on the first aid course at college, but panic creates a huge vacuum in my brain.

Check to see if the patient is still conscious.

I crouch down beside him.

'Dad... DAD... can you hear me?' I shout.

'Mmm...' he murmurs.

Is he conscious? Was that a "yes" or a groan of agony?

'CAN YOU HEAR ME, DAD?'

He opens his eyes. 'Of course I can hear you, you daft prick – you're bellowing down my bloody ear hole!'

He's definitely conscious!

I manage to get him into a sitting position just as Giant Haystacks appears with an ice-pack.

'Ambulance is on its way, mate,' he says.

'Cheers,' I reply as I apply the ice to the huge egg-shaped bump on dad's head.

'I'm fine,' announces dad, 'and I don't need a bloody ambulance.' He hauls himself to his feet and immediately falls over backwards, banging the back of his head against the stone step. He shouts out in pain, but instead of sympathy, I feel only anger. Why does he always have to play the hero?

'Dad, for once in your life, you're going to listen to me!' I yell. 'You're going in the ambulance and that's all there is to it.'

Dad peers up at me gratefully through drunken, concussed eyes and for the first time in my adult life, I feel some sort of connection between us.

russells hall

Richard: I hate hospitals. Back in the day, I came regularly to Russells Hall and it was always because of some unspeakable crime or another. I was forever interviewing obnoxious drunk-drivers, or pitiful victims of violence as they lay in their hospital beds. No wonder I can't stand the place. It doesn't help that my head feels like it's full of tiny miners tunnelling through my brain with pneumatic hammers, or that John keeps looking at me with a mixture of shock and disappointment. I want to say something to him, but I don't know what. I wish he'd stop looking at me like that. This is all Alice's fault. God, I hate her.

    John: This has gone from being a crap night to a really weird one. First the thing with Karen. I still can't get my head round that. And now this! What was dad doing in the nightclub? And since when does he *smoke*? I sneak a discreet look at him. He looks like shit.

    'Fancy a coffee from the machine?'

    He looks surprised. 'Thanks, son.' The faintest glimmer of a smile.

    I return five minutes later with two steaming cups of Styrofoam-flavoured water. We both take a sip and then shudder in simultaneous disgust. We look at each other and grin. Suddenly, the surrealism of the situation hits me; I'm sitting in hospital with my inebriated father after witnessing

95

him quite literally falling out of a nightclub and we're drinking coffee and smiling at each other and getting on better than we have done since... well since forever!

What the hell is going on here, John?

Dad shifts uncomfortably in his seat and clears his throat; I think I'm about to find out.

Richard: Strange. John's now being all amiable and sympathetic. I didn't expect that. The only problem is, the nicer he's being, the more I feel I should give him some sort of explanation. What do I tell him? I suppose I owe him the truth. I make myself as comfortable as possible in the hard-backed plastic chair and clear my throat.

'Tonight I was...' Bloody hell, this is more difficult than I thought, '...I was out with a woman.'

He looks at me as if I've just taken off my underpants and put them on my head. 'What? Like a date?'

I nod. He looks so hurt that I instantly regret telling him.

'So you're having an affair?'

'Technically, no. It was only a first date. Met her on the internet. Seemed like a nice girl...' John's the last person I ever thought I'd be baring my soul to, but now that I've started talking, I can't seem to stop. 'We met for a drink and then she said she wanted to go dancing. It went downhill from there. She was a complete psycho. Got me all hot under the collar and then acted like a hellcat when I responded amorously...'

John holds up his hands. 'Dad, please... spare me the gory details,' he begs.

'Yes, well, suffice to say, it didn't exactly go very well. I won't be seeing her again, so it's hardly the affair of the century, is it?'

John shakes his head in disbelief. 'That's not the point, dad,' he says, 'you were out with another woman – that's cheating in my book.'

His prissy "holier-than-thou" voice is really starting to piss me off and I have to remind myself that he is my son and that Alice is his mother. This can't be an easy conversation for him.

'Why would you cheat on mum?' he asks. The directness of the question temporarily throws me. I look at him, the innocence and naivety of his tender years are written on his young face. Can he handle the truth? Does he really want the truth? I decide that he deserves an honest answer. But which one? There's such a long list to choose from:

1. Your mother doesn't love me anymore.
2. She's having an affair with her yoga teacher.
3. She's only with me because of the inheritance money.
4. Every time I touch her in bed, she flinches and recoils from me.
5. I haven't had the balls to leave her and I hate myself for being so weak.
6. I haven't had sex in over a year.
7. I'm a man and I need sex.
8. Your mother wouldn't care if I fucked every woman in Dudley.
9. All of the above.

I eventually settle for a more diplomatic response. 'Your mother and me – we've been having a few problems.'

He rolls his eyes. 'What? You mean apart from the constant shouting and fighting?'

I shrug. 'Well, if you don't want to know.'

He sighs. 'Ok. What sort of problems?'

'Irreconcilable ones.'

'So you're finally getting a divorce?'

'Probably... eventually.'

'But in the meantime, you thought you'd go out and shag someone else?'

'No – that was your mother's response to the situation.'

He pauses as he processes this new information. 'She's shagging someone else?'

'She's rogering Roger.'

'The gay yoga bloke?!'

I nod grimly. 'Not so gay... apparently.'

'Shit,' says John.

'Shit,' I agree.

John: It's so bloody hot in here. Why is it so hot? I can feel the sweat dribbling down my spine and pooling somewhere down by my boxer shorts. **MUM. IS. HAVING. AN. AFFAIR.** The words are huge, bold and black and they fill up my head, squeezing everything else out.

'Shit...' I say. I'm too dazed and hot to think of a more appropriate response. Strangely, the word seems to offer dad some comfort. He smiles at me and shrugs.

'Shit,' he repeats.

As angry as I am at my mother, I can't see it as a personal betrayal. It's dad she's cheated on, not me.

'So, how are you... feeling?' I ask him.

'What about? The headache or being cuckolded by your mother?'

I consider this for a moment. 'Both.'

Richard: How am I feeling? Normally, I'd make some flippant remark involving water and a duck's back, but tonight something stops me. It's a long time since someone asked me how I felt. I try to remember the last time a person looked at me with such concern and enquired after my feelings. A memory slowly struggles up through the fug of my mind and settles in my throbbing consciousness. A dank, narrow corridor in a seedy little flat. The bathroom door, half open. My hand, trembling, on the doorknob. The stench of a decomposing body. The horror of the rotting greenish mass in the bathtub. Vomit... my own... in a warm pool on the bathroom floor. My face reflected back at me in the mirror above the sink... young and deathly pale. The kindly face of my superior officer, his eyes shining with compassion... 'You all right, son?'

I turn to John. 'I feel pretty crap, to be honest.'

My words surprise even me. John nods in sympathy and we sit for a moment in semi-companionable silence. A pretty young nurse enters the waiting room and calls my name. I get shakily to my feet, but John remains seated. He looks like he's about to cry and I feel suddenly sorry for the lad. I put a hand on his shoulder.

'Sorry, son. Maybe I should have kept my mouth shut. Drink does that to me, loosens my tongue.'

He shrugs and stands up. 'No, I'm glad you told me. You needed to tell someone.' He puts his arm around me so that he's supporting my weight. 'We'd better go and get that head of yours seen to.'

I lean into him, gratefully. My son, John.

John: I collapse on my bed, exhausted. The birds are singing and a hazy light filters through my curtains, but still I can't sleep. Poor dad. Deceived, betrayed, injured, bruised and hurting. I can't believe mum's done this to him. I mean, obviously, I know they don't have the easiest of relationships, but that's just how they've always been. Tonight has been a real eye-opener. He did a good job of maintaining his tough guy front, but I've never seen him so raw and exposed. All my life he's been a name to live up to, a force to be reckoned with, a father to be proud of. A giant of a man, a colossus, a leader. A dad? Rarely. A hero? Most definitely. When I was a kid, I really did think he was superman. Tall, muscular and good-looking, I was always being told about his valiant deeds at work – the dangerous criminals he'd nicked and the drug rings he'd busted. All I ever wanted to do was prove to him that I was a worthy son; that I was as strong, as athletic and as courageous as he was.

As a kid, learning to ride my bike, I was determined to make him proud by showing him I could do it on my own. Every evening I'd wait until he was sitting in his favourite armchair reading the newspaper and then I'd take my bike out onto the driveway. Dad's chair was in the bay window overlooking the front garden, so I knew he'd have a good view of me from there. For about a week I tried my hardest to impress him; getting straight back on every time I fell off, not crying when I grazed my knees, refusing to admit defeat when I struggled to maintain my balance. *If at first you don't succeed, try, try and try again!* Although I never did learn to ride it on my own, I wanted him to see how brave and persistent I was being. Fat chance! He never once looked up from his paper. He knew how desperate I was to win his approval, to hear his pompous words, 'Well done, son – that was very tenacious of you', and he was buggered if he was going to give me the satisfaction. I think it must have irritated him that I was so eager to please; he would probably have preferred a son who was more headstrong and independent. The ironic thing is, now that I am following my own path in life, he's still not happy because it doesn't fit in with his notion of success. He's a bloody difficult man! I wonder if things will change between us after tonight. When his head clears, will he regret what he told me? I'm not sure. But then again, I'm not sure of anything right now. Mum's having an affair and dad seems to be falling apart. My world will never be the same again.

a woman scorned

Richard: I've finally given in to the disgusting self-pity that's been threatening to swamp me for months. I'm wallowing, sinking and drowning in it. I'm not proud, but why not? My headache is monstrous and relentless and my marriage is on the brink of collapse. My lowest point was on Saturday morning when I was forced to confront Alice's wrath. She didn't believe for one minute my "I-fell-off-the-stepladder-whilst-changing-a-light-bulb" story.

'So, despite a deep gash to your head and a sprained ankle, you still managed to put away the stepladder and remove all traces of blood before the paramedics arrived?' she remarked, po-faced. Distrustful cow. Infuriatingly, her acerbic wit reminded me of why I fell in love with her in the first place. God, I hate her. I spent a miserable weekend in bed, in accordance with the doctor's strict instructions.

'You're a lucky man, Mr Harrison,' she informed me, 'you could have been very seriously injured.' To be fair, I hardly call cracking my head open and twisting my ankle after a humiliatingly unsuccessful attempt at an extra-marital affair "lucky", but I suppose I can see her point. So although I feel physically and emotionally annihilated, I'm trying to cheer myself up by telling myself that things could be even worse. So far, it's not working.

John: Karen's waiting for me in the foyer when I get into college this morning.

'John, can I have a word?' she asks. I assume she wants to apologise for Friday night, but I never want to speak to the mad bitch again. I try to smile.

'No need,' I tell her, 'everything's fine.'

Her jowls wobble in indignation. 'I'm afraid there's *every* need,' she insists, 'and everything is most definitely *not* "fine"!'

She turns smartly on her heel and click-clacks across the wide entrance hall towards a small interview room off the reception area. As I follow her into the room, my heart flips and quivers like a dying fish on the deck of boat. It takes all my strength to close the door and face her.

Hell hath no fury...

I recoil in shock as I find myself face-to-face with Simon from HR. He's the guy who interviewed me. What the hell is he doing here? Karen sits next to him and motions for me to sit opposite them.

'Look, what is all this about?' I demand.

'Please John, there's no need to be rude.'

Karen sits back, a smug smile sitting atop her double chin. I look into those hateful eyes and I can see she's enjoying every second of this.

'What *is* your problem, Karen?'

Her eyes narrow. 'Be very, *very* careful about how you speak to me, John.'

'I have absolutely nothing to say to you,' I tell her with equal venom.

Smarmy Simon coughs politely and holds up a placatory hand. 'It's OK, John. You have a right to remain silent.'

Who does this joker think he is? Inspector fucking Morse?

'Look, Karen' I say, 'I have no idea what all this is about, but I've got nothing to hide. I've never been anything but professional.'

Karen swivels slowly and mechanically in my direction, like a primitive stop-motion animation. The snakes on her head flick their evil tongues at me. 'If you're so *professional* John, why do you think it is that you're being suspended from work?'

Her Medusa stare turns me to stone.

Richard: Stephen Hawking, David Blunkett, David Mellor, John Prescott, Sven Goran Eriksson... all notably unattractive men who've had affairs with young, attractive women. I'm not sure where I'm going with this train of thought, but it's doing nothing to restore my damaged ego.

John: I practically run out of building, mobile phone at the ready, desperate to talk to her. I find a bench in a nearby street and call her. She answers with her habitual 'Hey, handsome.'

'I have to tell you something,' I say, 'about one of my students.'

'Not again,' she groans, 'I don't think I can take another "amusing" anecdote or "inspirational" story of triumph over adversity.'

'This is serious, Sarah,' I say and something in my voice makes her shut up and listen.

'I've been accused of kissing a female student.' The line goes quiet. 'It's a lie,' I add quickly, 'but it's her word against mine.' Her silence is so complete that I assume she's hung up.

'Sarah? Are you still there.'

'Yes.'

'It's a lie, Sarah,' I repeat. 'I'd never do a thing like that and I'd never cheat on you. I love you.' The words are out of my mouth before I've even had time to think about them.

I've never told her that I love her before and I realise with sudden startling clarity that I do. That I always have.

'What's her name?' she asks quietly.

'Jaya,' I reply. 'Not that it matters. Did you hear what I said? I love you.'

'I love you too,' she says matter-of-factly, as if it's so self-evident that it hardly warrants mentioning. Suddenly I need to tell her everything. About Friday night, Karen, my dad's disastrous date, my mum's affair... everything.

'Sarah, we need to talk.'

Richard: How do other people go about it? They all seem to be at it. You can't open a paper or switch on the TV without hearing about everyone else's sordid affairs. Is that what I even want? A sordid affair? It's true, I need sex, but am I really willing to pay the price? I can definitely do without the ritual humiliation of dating women like Jayde. What was I even *thinking*? And what the *fuck* am I still doing with Alice? I ask myself that question every day. I know I don't love her any more. I'm not financially dependent on her, or emotionally tied to her. So what is it that's keeping me from packing my bags and getting the hell out of here? I think, more than anything, it's the fear of the unknown. Being married is so much a part of my identity that I can't envisage myself any other way. A married, middle-aged, middle-class male. That's who I am. It suits me and defines me: solid, dependable, serious... married. What's the alternative? Single. Divorced. Sad. Lonely. Living in a bachelor pad, breath stinking of stale beer, wearing the same underpants for three days in a row. That's just not how I see myself. So where does that leave me? Trapped in a stale, loveless marriage until death us do part, I suppose. She'll never leave me. She's got it too good. Money, status, a big house, a villa in Spain, as many hair and nail appointments as she can cram into her bulging social diary. I doubt Roger's got a pot to piss in. His type are all the same. It's all peace and fucking love and let some other poor bastard pick up the tab. Hippy fucking prick. *Christ* my head hurts. I really need to get laid.

John: I walk into the living room at 11 o' clock in the morning to find dad slumped in his armchair. My own worries are temporarily forgotten as I crouch down beside him.

'Dad! Are you OK?'

He mumbles something incomprehensible about Stephen Hawking and his head lolls to the side. As I stand there briefly contemplating how dad will take to life in a mental institution, he suddenly looks up at me and barks, 'What the bloody hell are you doing home from work? And what's wrong with you? You look like shit!' And so I tell him. Talking to Sarah seems to have opened the floodgates and I tell him all about Jaya and Karen and what happened today. The words pour out of me and, as I talk, I notice dad taking more and more notice and becoming increasingly alert. When I finish the whole sorry story, he gets up and grabs a notebook and pen from a drawer.

'Right,' he says. 'Start again from the beginning. And this time, I'm making notes.'

Richard: So I've finally found out why John's been acting so strangely for the last few weeks. He's a complete fool for letting it happen. It seems he was aware that this girl was infatuated by him and did nothing about it. I don't like the sound of this Karen woman either. Seems like she could be out to get him. There's no proof of it of course, but it certainly doesn't bode well. It looks like my lad could be in seriously hot water here.

John: Strangely, I think the trouble I'm in at work has actually cheered dad up. Well, maybe that's a bit unfair, but he's definitely acting more like his old self again. The only difference is, we're actually communicating with each other and this time, he's not drunk and concussed. This is the longest conversation we've ever had without one of us shouting (usually him) or storming off (usually me). He's listening intently to everything I'm saying, pausing only to scribble down facts in his notebook. After the second time I've recounted the story he looks at me and clears his throat.

'I want to get this completely straight,' he begins. 'Karen was waiting for you when you got to work this morning?' He looks up and I nod. 'She informed you that Jaya had made a serious allegation against you and that you were being suspended from work until further notice?'

'Yes,' I confirm. 'That's when I said I had a right to know what allegation had been made.'

'Quite right,' agrees my father as he makes another note in his book, 'and her exact words were...?'

'She said that Jaya said we were "boyfriend and girlfriend" and that I'd kissed her in the disabled toilets at college.'

'Do you know why Jaya would say something like that?'

'No.'

Come on, John – be honest.

'Well, between you and me, I may have been a bit over familiar – put my arm around her shoulder, that sort of thing. She must have got the wrong end of the stick.'

'But you definitely never kissed her?'

I can feel the colour rising in my cheeks as I burn with embarrassment and anger.

'Dad, do you really need to ask? I was only ever nice to her. I would never take advantage of a girl!' Tears prick the backs of my eyes. 'I wanted to... to help her, not seduce her, for crying out loud!'

Dad puts down his notebook and looks at me with...
with affection, I think. He stretches out his arm and for one
awful moment I think he's going to hug me. Instead, he
leans over and ruffles my hair, in a somewhat awkward, yet
fatherly gesture.

'John, I'm your dad. I know you. I'm only trying to
ascertain the facts.' I nod, feeling calmer. 'So Karen then
asked you to leave the premises, is that right?'

'Yeah.' I still can't quite believe this is happening.
'Christ dad, what am I going to do?'

He smiles. 'Don't worry son', he says, 'I know plenty
of good lawyers.'

I return the smile. I suppose having a father who's a
policeman does have its advantages.

decision time

John: I'm in such deep shit. Why didn't I see this coming? I knew she had a crush on me. I just assumed it was the sort of crush that a ten-year-old would have on her big brother's best mate. Why did I assume that? Because she has a learning difficulty? Did I lead her on, then? I remember feeling sorry for her when Karen made a big deal about her fancying me. So maybe I over-compensated with all the touchy-feely stuff? Nah. I don't think I even considered her feelings at all.

'You getting 'em in or what?' Cameron's booming voice brings me back to the here and now.

'Sorry, mate, what was it again?'

'For fuck's sake, Johno!' My best mate rolls his eyes for dramatic effect. 'We've been drinking together since we were sixteen. What's wrong with you?'

'Do you really want to know?'

Somehow I doubt it. Cam and me don't do the "heart-to-heart" thing. With us it's all about beer, footie and birds. As predicted, he shrugs noncommitally and I turn back towards the bar.

We take our drinks over to the pool table and I watch Cam rack up the balls. Really, it's no wonder Jaya got confused. All that hugging and hand holding; my conduct was, at best, insensitive and, at worst, cruel.

So why did you do it, John?

Good question. I know I didn't fancy her and I like to think I'm not such a weak character that I was flattered by the attention. In fact, I don't think I even thought about Jaya as a person at all. I think her learning difficulty made her somehow sexless in my eyes; an innocent, childlike being, incapable of passion or romantic feeling.

'Your break wasn't it?'

'Eh?'

'Look, Johno – we may as well just call it a night.' Cameron doesn't look best pleased.

'What you on about?' I ask him. 'I was waiting for you to rack 'em up!'

'The thing is mate,' he says, 'you've hardly said two words to me all night and now you're mooning round the place like a wet bloody lettuce.'

'Let's just play,' I sigh, as I snatch one of the cues out of his hand. He looks at me with genuine concern.

'Look, I'm not very good at this sort of stuff,' he mumbles awkwardly, 'but if you want to get something off your chest.'

I'm surprised and touched by his offer and I suppose I can't keep such a major personal crisis a secret from him forever.

'I'm in a bit of bother at work,' I say.

'Oh yeah?'

'Yeah. In fact, I've been suspended.'

'No shit?! Why? What did you do?'

To be honest, Cameron's the last person I would ever confide in. He's got a bigger gob than most of the girls I know.

'Nothing! Well, not what I've been accused of, anyway,' I assure him, 'but I can't really go into it.'

'Jesus, sounds serious.'

'It is. Sorry I can't say any more, mate.'

'Fair enough.'

'There is something I'd like to talk to you about, though.'

'Go on...'

Cameron and his girlfriend, Sam, have been together since they were thirteen and they're the most solid couple I know. He obviously knows the secret of a good relationship and I could use his advice.

'I've done some things I'm not proud of,' I begin. He looks at me keenly, his gossip-sensors clearly aroused. 'The thing is,' I continue, 'my conscience is niggling me and I don't know whether to come clean with Sarah.'

'You and your bloody conscience,' grins Cam.

'Yeah, I know,' I say apologetically. 'So, what would you do?'

'You haven't cheated on her?'

'No! It's to do with this thing at work.'

'I thought you said you hadn't done anything wrong?'

'Well, I have and I haven't. Maybe I'm being too harsh on myself, but I don't feel I've been very...,' I search for the right word, '...chivalrous, I suppose.'

Cam laughs. 'Chivalry's dead, man. It's all about that PC bollocks nowadays.'

'Yeah, well, I haven't been that either.'

'What exactly have you done, mate?' I hesitate as I weigh up how much I can tell him.

'I've treated someone badly. Disrespectfully. A girl.'

'And?'

'If you were in my shoes, would you tell Sam?'

'You must be joking!'

I'm shocked – I really thought they told each other everything.

'What? Even if you felt really guilty?'

111

'*Especially* if I felt really guilty.'

'But you two are always banging on about honesty and openness in your relationship.'

'No, that's what Sam says,' he corrects, 'I just go along with it to keep her happy.'

'So, what you're saying is—'

'Look,' he interrupts, 'I'm not saying you should cheat and lie. I'd never do that to Sam. I love her. I'm just saying keep your battles with your conscience to yourself.'

I sigh. Maybe he's right. But then, could I actually live with myself? Cam holds up his pool cue and waggles it warningly in the air.

'Now stop thinking about it, whatever it is, and let's play some pool!'

'So I definitely shouldn't tell Sarah?'

'No effin' way!'

OK. So maybe I won't tell Sarah.

Richard: Jack slams back his second double whiskey and wipes his mouth with the back of his hand. I know how he feels. I shouldn't even be back at work. I can hardly put any pressure on my ankle and my eye's still half closed. On top of that, it's been a bastard of a day and our investigation into the child rape case on the Wren's Nest has sent us both to the bottom of the bottle tonight. It takes a lot to shock me nowadays, but the events of today have been particularly harrowing. There was a time when I found every violent crime emotionally upsetting. I turn to my friend and colleague of twenty years.

'Do you remember my first murder case?' I ask him. Jack looks back at me through hazy eyes and nods vaguely before ordering another double. It had been a young Asian girl – a so called "honour" killing. She was only fifteen – a lovely looking kid. Strangled and stabbed by her father and two brothers.

'You cried like a baby,' says Jack, putting voice to my thoughts.

'*Precisely,*' I agree.

If Jack is puzzled by this remark, he doesn't show it. He's the only person I've entrusted with the real reason for my injuries. Everyone else at work got the same "changing a light-bulb" bollocks as Alice.

'What I want to know is,' I ask, directing my question at the glass in my hand, 'at what point did I become *this* man. A man who can discuss footie results over the body of a suicide victim?'

Jack shrugs. 'You've got to be hard in this game. It's an occupational necessity.'

'True. But I always thought I was fundamentally unchanged.'

'In what way?'

I think about John. Wrestling with his conscience, trying to rescue his integrity from the mess he's made of things. He's cocked up big time, but at least he's trying to be honest with himself. When was the last time I was honest with myself?

'Well, that I was still the idealistic kid who joined the force to "make a difference".'

Jack raises his glass in a drunken salute. 'I'll drink to that!'

'But the thing is, Jack,' I struggle to focus on my own words; what am I banging on about? 'The thing is... I'm not that man anymore.'

'Of course you're not – you're a tough son of a bitch.'

I shake my head. I've only to look at John to be reminded of the man I used to be. The man I could be again. If I tried.

'But I'm not. I mean I am, but I don't want to be anymore.'

Jack looks uncomfortable at the turn the conversation has taken. 'What are you saying, you mad bastard?' he asks, gruff, yet affectionate.

I smile as I am suddenly hit by a moment of complete lucidity.

'What I'm saying, Jack my old pal, is... I quit.'

the break-up

John: I'm crying, wailing, pleading into the phone. 'Sarah, *please* don't do this!'

'You've left me with no choice,' she says sadly.

'But, there's no need to end it—'

'How did you expect me to react?'

'I don't know,' I reply, 'I guess I'd hoped you'd understand.'

'Well I don't, John. I don't understand how you could play with the emotions of a vulnerable young woman... a young woman *in your care*!' In all the time we've been together, this is the first time I've ever heard her raise her voice in real anger.

'I didn't do it deliberately,' I protest, 'but, looking back, I can see how I might have inadvertently encouraged her. I didn't *actually* do anything wrong, but I wanted to be totally honest with you.'

'You didn't *actually* do anything wrong?' she repeats. 'How can you say that?'

'Because I didn't realise what I was doing.'

'That's no excuse. You're pathetic. I never want to see you again.'

'*Please!*'

'You make me sick!'

The line goes dead. I stare at the silent phone in my hand. It's probably for the best. In fact, it's a suitably fitting punishment for my crime. I don't deserve a girlfriend like Sarah. I'm not worthy of her love. Not after what I've done.

Richard: 'Are you out of your tiny little mind?!' Her eyes flash dangerously. I realise she's being insulting, but still I ponder the question.

'No – I don't think so.'

'What about the mortgage?'

'There's only a year left on it,' I remind her. 'Anyway, you could always get a job.'

'*Me* get a job!?' she splutters.

'I might sell the villa, or even the house. I could always upsize again when the inheritance comes through.'

She stares at me incredulously. 'But that could be years!' she shrieks.

'I certainly hope so,' I agree. I've no wish to see mum and dad kick the bucket just yet.

'What about John? Think about your son!'

'Well, at some point he'll be in line to inherit over a million quid, so I'm sure he'll be just fine.'

'That's all well and good, but what about now?'

'Well he's not working at the moment. Maybe we could all go backpacking together?' I chuckle to myself as I picture Alice sleeping rough and eating bush tucker in the Australian outback. 'There's a thought, eh?'

'Have you gone totally fucking crazy?!'

'No – in fact, this is the sanest I've felt in a long time.'

'No!' she says, shaking her head, wildly. 'I won't let you do it!'

I take her gently by the shoulders. 'Alice,' I say, 'I already have.'

John: I don't know how long I've been sitting on my bed, cradling the phone, but at some point the birds stopped singing and the sun set. I think I must be cold as there are goose bumps on my bare arms. My parents have been home for a while, but neither of them have bothered putting the central heating on. Mum sounds like she's about to start Frisbeeing the china again at any moment. It's always been the same with those two. When I was a kid, they were always either snogging one another's faces off or hurling bedroom furniture at each other. Nowadays they don't bother with the kissing and making up, they just stick to the full-on nightly onslaught. I always dreamed of a more stable relationship, which is why I fell for Sarah. She's so grounded and laid-back – there's never any drama with Sarah. Well, none of her making anyway. What am I going to do without her? How will I cope with the regular domestic warfare in my living room without our soothing post-barney conversations? How will I see the funny side of my dad's lectures or my mum's mood swings without her cheerful psychoanalysis of my fucked-up family? Without her, my life is an unbearable circus act and it stretches out before me – melodramatic, freakish and excruciating.

Richard: She's off to her sister's, thank God. I'm getting too old for all this. Maybe we should just call it a day. She can have half of everything, I don't care anymore. I'll talk to her tomorrow – see what she says. Strangely, I don't feel too bad. I think I'm still on a high from handing in my notice. I'm a free man! Free to do whatever I want. The world is my oyster. I remember when Alice and I first got together – we had so many plans. We were going to make love in every capital city in Europe. She was such a wild child. Fierce and intense... but sweet and vulnerable too. For months she would cry every time I entered her. Her dark eyes would lock onto mine and I'd watch them fill with tears. Fat, angry tears, which tasted of sex and freedom. God she was beautiful back then. My beautiful, angry girl. I thought I would be the one to soothe and pacify her, but instead her rage has grown with every year of our marriage. Of course she's changed; she's lost the energy and wanderlust of her youth. But the anger has never gone away. Well, enough is enough. I can't do this anymore. Something's got to give and it's not going to be me. I will not let Alice poison the rest of my life with her toxic words and venomous looks. From now on, happiness is my one and only goal.

John: Mum falls through my bedroom door, blubbing and snivelling. I hear her fingernails scrabbling on the wall as she searches for the light-switch.

'Mum?' I call out. She flicks on the light and we stare at each other across the room with similarly moist, startled eyes.

'John?' She wipes her grey tears on her sleeve. 'What are you doing sitting in the dark?'

'What are you doing in my bedroom?' I ask.

'Looking for my suitcase,' she replies. I point to the corner of the room where it stands, still stuffed with dirty laundry from my last weekend in London.

'Off to Roger's?' I ask. She looks up sharply. It's the first time I've ever mentioned the bastard's name. 'Well? Are you?' I ask hoarsely. I could do with a good fight myself. She crosses the room and sits on the end of my bed.

'My baby,' she murmurs, running her painted talons through my hair.

'Don't, mum.' I pull away and lean against the wall, eyeing her suspiciously. She looks tired. 'Are you going to leave dad?' I ask her.

She sighs. 'I don't know. Yes... I think so.'

'Do you love Roger?'

'It's complicated,' she replies.

'No it's not,' I snap, 'either you love him or you don't.'

118

She shrugs infuriatingly and allows her eyes to roam about my bedroom, resting on my collectable *Star Wars* toys on the shelf above my bed.

'You're still so young, baby boy,' she says, 'what do you know about love?'

Baby boy?! I feel affronted. Patronised. I open my mouth to put her straight. Then I stop and think about Sarah and about Jaya.

She's right, John. What do you know?

'Nothing,' I whisper hollowly, 'I know nothing about love.' We sit there in wretched chumminess, united in our misery.

'I always believed in "The One",' she says suddenly, breaking the silence. 'I really thought that one day I'd find the man of my dreams.'

I've never heard her talk like this before, but I can't be her shoulder to cry on.

'Yeah? Well shit happens,' I reply.

My mother gives a bitter laugh. 'It certainly does, my darling, it certainly does.'

the morning after

John: I push my cornflakes around the bowl and watch them disintegrate into the slushy milk. This week just keeps getting better and better. First Sarah dumps me, then dad quits his job and then mum buggers off to Auntie Helen's. Mum reckons dad's gone nuts and that he's off to live in some hippie commune. Not sure if she's joking or not. Why can't he just have a normal midlife crisis like every other old bloke? I hear him humming as he walks into the kitchen and he joins me at the breakfast bar. He flashes me a big beaming grin and it dawns on me that this is the happiest I've ever seen him.

'Alright son?' he asks, as he unfolds his morning paper. 'Any news from the college?'

'No,' I reply, 'don't think I'll hear anything until after the Christmas holidays now.'

'Chin up, eh mate?' he says and turns his attention to his paper.

'Yeah. Chin up.' I stare miserably into my soggy cornflakes. 'Have you heard from mum?'

Dad frowns and looks up at me. 'Look mate, me and your mum. We, we erm—'

'It's OK, dad,' I tell him, 'you don't have to go into it.'

He looks relieved. 'Well, if you want to talk things through, then I'm—'

'Sarah's dumped me,' I blurt out.

'No!' he looks genuinely gutted. 'I thought you said she was going to stand by you?'

'Yeah, well, that was before I told her the whole truth.'

'The whole truth?'

'You know, about the way I led Jaya on and everything.'

Dad puts down his paper. 'John, don't you think you're going a bit over-the-top with this guilty conscience thing?'

'Not really,' I reply, 'I've been a total bastard.'

He rolls his eyes. 'Well maybe by your own impossibly high standards,' he says.

'What do you mean?'

'Well, as far as I can tell, you've been incredibly stupid and naïve.'

'Nice one. Thanks.'

'But you've nothing else to reproach yourself for.'

'How can you say that, dad?'

'Come on, John, you didn't deliberately set out to seduce or manipulate her, did you?'

'No.'

Dad looks me squarely in the eyes. 'So what are you actually guilty of?'

'I called her "sweetheart".'

He raises his eyes heavenward. 'Oh pur-lease!'

'I... I didn't once stop to consider her feelings.'

'OK, so you were overfamiliar and thoughtless. Hardly the crime of the century, is it? Can't you just put it down to your own inexperience and move on?'

'But I feel so guilty, dad,' I wail, sounding like an adolescent girl, even to my own ears.

'For pity's sake John,' he snaps, 'stop feeling so damn sorry for yourself!' That sounds more like the dad I know.

Instinctively, I make to leave, but he puts a conciliatory hand on my shoulder.

'Look, mate,' he says, 'it wasn't premeditated and you never laid a finger on her, right?' I nod and sit back down. 'Whereas *she*,' he continues, 'has made a totally false allegation against you. One that could cost you your job.'

He's got a point. So why do I feel so shit?

'If I was you, John,' he continues, 'I'd get on the phone to that little lass of yours and I'd be on the next train to London.'

'Thanks dad,' I say, 'but she doesn't want to know.'

'Then she's a fool,' he replies. 'She'll never find a better bloke than you.'

Richard: Out of the blue, John slams into me. For a split second, I think he's rugby tackling me, but then his arms go around my shoulders and I realise... it's a hug. The sensation is unfamiliar and pleasant. For a moment I'm taken aback, quite literally, and I teeter on the back legs of my chair. But then I take in the sweet scent of his hair and I'm rewarded with the memory of his frequent childhood embraces. The smell is less "damp pup" and more "groomed male" than it used to be, but it's still unmistakably the smell of my little boy.

'Thanks dad,' he croaks, but I'm too overcome to reply.

John: I make two coffees to allow us both time to recover.

'So how are you, dad?' I ask, placing a steaming mug in front of him. 'How are you, *really*?'

'Not bad, considering,' he says. 'In fact, I didn't realise just how much the job was getting me down.' He grins at me. 'Should have quit years ago.'

'So what are you going to do?'

'Exactly what I said,' he replies, 'downsize and live off the money from this place for a bit.'

'So you're not going backpacking?'

He chuckles. 'You been speaking to your mother?'

I nod guiltily.

'Of course I'm not, you daft sod,' he says, 'and there'll always be a place for you in the new house.'

'Mum too?'

He stiffens. 'I don't know about that.'

'She seemed pretty upset last night.'

'Yeah? Well, like I said, I'm going to live by my own rules from now on. Your mum can like it or lump it.'

I don't push it, but it occurs to me that this really is the end of the road for my parents.

'What about you?' he asks. 'Have you thought about what you'll do if... if things don't go your way at work?'

'If they sack me, you mean?'

He nods. 'Shall I give Bruce a call?'

I shoot him a warning glance.

'Sorry, bad joke.' He smiles sadly. 'You'll never be able to work in education again, you know.'

'Yeah, thanks for reminding me.'

'You need to be prepared for the worst.'

I think about Sarah. Her kindness, her cheeriness, her beautiful smile. 'The worst has already happened, dad.'

PART THREE
JAYA

'Sometimes the lies you tell are less frightening than the loneliness you might feel if you stopped telling them.'

Brock Clarke

the dream

I'm sitting in the bath dreaming of John. I really miss him because mum won't let me go to college and he isn't my friend on Facebook anymore. I think he must have unfriended me after I sent him the letter. I was really upset, but I know he didn't want to do it. They made him. I don't know why everyone is so annoyed about the letter. But maybe I shouldn't have told Karen that I kissed John in the toilet. I only said it because she kept going on about personal space again and it made me angry because I can go out with whoever I like. I'm an adult now and I can kiss who I want to and I can have sex with who I want to too. Mum told me all about men and sex and stuff ages ago and she said it was a nice thing to do with someone that you love. Well I love John and I want to marry him. I'm really worried in case I never see him again. Maybe I should go to his house? I know where he lives because there's a picture of him on Facebook standing outside his front door and the street name is actually on the wall of his house. Perhaps we should run away? Then no-one can stop us being together. We can get married and have sex and have lots of babies. I love him so much. I think about him all the time, especially when I touch myself down there. I touch myself now and I think of John. I think about all the things we'll do in bed together when we're married. All the things I've seen in magazines and on the internet. I'm lying in John's arms. They're strong and warm around me. I feel his breath against my ear. It tickles. He puts his tongue inside my ear, which makes me gasp and wriggle around. It feels so nice that it sort of hurts, but it doesn't. I push myself against him. He holds me tighter and I feel something hard against my leg. I know what it is. It is his penis. His penis is hard, which means he wants to have sex with me. I know what to do. I open my legs wide so he can put his hard penis into my vagina. This is sex. I am having sex with John. We are having sex with each other. John and me. Having sex. Making love. Fucking. "Fuck" is a very, *very* bad swear word, but it also means sex, so it's OK to say "fuck" if you're talking about sex. I can feel tingling down below. It's getting stronger and is moving up into my belly. I can't breathe properly and I'm panting like a puppy dog. John whispers I love you Jaya in my ear. The tingling turns into fireworks which bang and whizz up and down my body. I scream and scream and scream. Then mum bangs on the bathroom door and shouts are you OK Jaya? I shout back yes I'm fine and she says don't lock the bloody door when you're in the bath, don't you know you could drown? I say yes sorry to shut her up, but I don't unlock the bathroom door because it's my private time. Sometimes mum can be a real pain. I wish she'd just leave me alone. It's her fault I can't see John any more. I love her and I don't want her to be sad, but I love John too. I want to be with him so much. I dream about him every day and every night. I dream about kissing him and touching him and doing everything else with him. I say his name and touch myself again. John. John. John. John. John. Mum starts banging on the bathroom door again. Unlock the door Jaya. Unlock the bloody door. Why can't she just go away? I slide down deeper into the bath and let the water go over my head.

the lie

Mum stares at me and says what did you say? I say it again in case she didn't hear, but actually I think she did hear and is just pretending that she didn't. Mum is still staring at me and not saying anything, which is really weird. Then she gets up off the sofa and walks to the TV and then back to the sofa and sits down again. Then her body goes stiff and her eyes bulge out really far and she grabs my hand and it hurts. I say mum you're hurting me but she doesn't let go and I feel a bit frightened, even though she's my mum. She opens her mouth and I think she's going to say something but instead she starts breathing really fast like she's hurt herself. Then I say, mum are you OK? And she says, what the hell are you talking about, Jaya? What the hell do you mean you had sex with John? When did it happen? You've been at home with me all week. I'm so angry at mum because she keeps going on at me all the time and won't give me five minutes peace. So to shut her up, I told her John came over and we had sex. I thought it would make her see that I'm really serious about him, but now I wish I hadn't lied. Mum squeezes my hand even tighter and shouts, Jaya I asked you a question, when did it happen? And then I tell another lie, but I only say it to make her let go of me because now her nails are digging into my skin and there is blood on my hand. I tell her he came over when she went to Tesco with Bee. I say we still love each other and want to get married and please let go of my hand mum because you're really hurting me. So mum lets go of my hand and then she goes all droopy and her head flops onto her chest, which is even scarier than when she was angry. She gets up really slowly, walks over to the phone, picks it up and dials a number. Then she says, police please. I don't know why she's calling the police, but I don't like it and I shout at her to stop. Then she turns to me and screams SHUT UP, JAYA in a loud, horrible voice that doesn't sound like hers and so I shut up. Then she turns back to the phone and says yes, hello, police? I'd like to report a rape.

the policewoman

The policewoman is really scary and keeps asking me loads
of questions. Mum is sitting next to me and she looks
angry, but I'm not sure if she's angry with me or not. The
policewoman says did you invite John into your house,
Jaya? I tell her yes. Then she asks, why did you invite John
in? I tell her because I love him and I wanted to see him.
Then she says what happened when you invited John in? I
say, we had sex. Mum gets up and shouts THE BASTARD
really loudly and the policewoman says I know this is very
hard for you Mrs Jones but please try to remain calm. Then
mum says how can I be calm when my daughter's been
raped? And the policewoman says we're still trying to
establish whether that is actually the case. Then mum goes
really mental and shouts of course it's the bloody case,
she's a vulnerable adult and he's her bloody care worker,
what else would you call it if it's not rape? Then the
policewoman says let's have a five minute break shall we?
And she goes out to make us all a cup of tea. She comes
back and we drink our tea and then she asks me some more
questions. She's much nicer this time and her voice is softer
and more friendly. She says, do you know what sex is,
Jaya? I say yes I do, it's when a man puts his penis in a
woman's vagina. Then she says, and is that what John did
to you? And I say yes. Then mum starts to cry and I tell her

131

not to be sad. I take her hand and I tell her John and me are going to get married and it's OK for a man and a woman to have sex if they're going to get married. I tell her everything is going to be OK. I'm not sure why, but this makes mum cry even more. The policewoman waits for mum to stop crying and then asks me if I wanted to have sex with John and I say yes. Then the policewoman gets up and says she's very sorry but it seems that no crime has actually been committed. Then she uses lots of big words that I don't understand and I don't know what she's talking about, so I ask her to explain. She says I'm telling your mum that I think you and John wanted to have sex with each other, which means you haven't been raped. Then she asks me if I understand and I say yes and I feel happy because it means John won't get into trouble. Then mum asks, so it's OK for a teacher to take advantage of a vulnerable adult in his care, is it? The policewoman says no of course not. Then she uses lots of big words again and I don't know what she's saying, but it doesn't sound very nice. Then I get scared again that she's going to arrest John, so I ask her if she is and she says no. So then mum grabs the policewoman's hand and says please, please help us. The policewoman looks really sad and pats mum's hand. Mum grabs the policewoman's other hand and says please, you have to do something because she doesn't understand what's happened to her. That makes me feel really sad but I don't know why. Then the policewoman asks mum to let go of her hands and says that she'll definitely be having a word with Mr Harrison and with the principal of the college. So I get really angry and stand up and shout at her to leave John alone because it's none of her business and I don't want John to be in trouble. So mum yells, just bloody sit down Jaya, will you? Then she says sorry about that, just ignore her, she doesn't know what she's saying. And the policewoman shakes her head and says I'm sorry but I'm afraid I have to disagree. She says Jaya seems to be a mature young woman who knows her own mind and I say yes I am. Mum shakes her head. No, she whispers, you've got it all wrong and you're going to let the bastard get away with it. Then the policewoman pats mum's shoulder and says I'm very sorry Mrs Jones and she goes away. Then mum and me are left on our own.

friends for life

Just let her go says Bee. Mum looks angry and I think she's going to tell her to keep her nose out but she doesn't. Bee gives mum a hug and says look I know you're going through hell right now but keeping Jaya locked in the house isn't helping anyone. Mum looks at me and then back at Bee and she looks like she's thinking about it. I haven't been out the house for three days so I really hope she says yes, even though I don't actually want to go. I love my Friends For Life group but Kerry Holt texted me yesterday and said she's going to get me. She said that John's been sacked from college and that everyone hates me. Then on Facebook she said she'd beat me up if I ever show my face at college or Friends For Life again. She said I got John the sack on purpose because he wouldn't go out with me, which is a lie but I don't care. I don't care because I feel so bad that nothing Kerry says can make me feel worse. Kerry is such a cow because when she cheated on Ian with Daniel McDonagh she made me swear not to tell and I didn't tell a soul. The only person I told was Holly Henson and that didn't count because she swore not to tell. When Ian found out and everyone was calling Kerry a slapper I was the only person who stuck up for her. I wish I hadn't bothered now. Mum and Bee are still talking about tonight and I know mum will say no because she's scared something bad will happen to me again. I really wish I hadn't lied about John but it's too late now. Then mum says OK you can go tonight but only if me and Bee drop you off and pick you up in the car. That means that Kishan will come too which is not good because he always sticks his head out the car window and shouts bye Jaya, bye Jaya, BYE JAYA. I know he's disabled and it's not his fault but sometimes I wish he wasn't so embarrassing.

In the car mum asks if Kerry Holt will be there tonight and I say yeah probably. So mum says well make sure you don't talk about you know who and I say OK mum. Then Kishan says OK mum, OK mum, OK MUM so I tell him to shut-up. I see mum and Bee looking at each other but they don't say anything. When we get there mum gives me a big kiss and says text me if you want us to pick you up early, but I tell her I'll be OK. When I walk in Kerry is already there but she ignores me and carries on talking to Greg Davies. She's such a slapper. I'm really glad that no-one else from college comes here because I actually really don't want to talk about John. I feel so bad that he got the sack because of me. Poor John. I go over and sit on the arts and crafts table because that's what I always do. Normally Kerry sits next to me and we make stuff together but tonight she's on the creative writing table. Edward Clarke is sitting opposite me making Christmas tree decorations. Every week he asks me to be his girlfriend and every week I say no. Ed is OK but he's quite fat and has a squeaky voice so I don't really fancy him. He knows everything there is to know about bus timetables and can tell you the number of any bus going anywhere in the West Midlands. He likes it if you ask him questions about buses because he always knows the answer. Hi Ed I say but he doesn't say hi back. I think maybe he didn't hear me so I ask him what number bus goes from Wolverhampton town centre to

Merry Hill. Ed looks up and whispers the 255 National Express bus goes from Wolverhampton bus station to Wombourne, Swindon, Kingswinford and Merry Hill, via Penn, Wall Heath, Bromley and Brierley Hill. Thanks Ed I say but why are you whispering? Ed looks over towards Kerry but she's laughing at something Greg just said. So Ed says really quietly that Kerry said no-one was supposed to talk to me because I was a slag and had got someone the sack. Sorry Jaya says Ed but Kerry made us all promise. Then Kerry looks over and sees Ed talking to me and gives him a dirty look. Ed puts his head down really quickly and pretends to sprinkle silver glitter on his snowman but I can see that the lid is still on the sprinkler. I pick up some red card and gold glitter and start making a Christmas card for mum. Then Kerry goes to the toilet and Ed gets up out of his seat and walks around the table to me. He says Jaya can I ask you a question? But I don't answer him because I'm still angry with him. Jaya will you be my girlfriend? asks Ed. No Ed I say. I finish my card for mum and start a new one for John. I draw mistletoe and a picture of us underneath it and spend ages doing the bubble writing so it looks really neat. Then I see Kerry coming over to the arts and crafts table and try to hide the card but it's too late. She snatches it out my hand and reads my message to John. Hey that's private I shout but Kerry just laughs. You're so stupid Jaya she says. John doesn't love you. He's got a girlfriend in London, everybody knows. That's a lie I say but I can feel my face going red and tears springing up out of my eyes. No it isn't says Kerry. Her name is Sarah. He told me about her ages ago in speaking and listening practice. Then Kerry Holt rips up my Christmas card and says Ha Ha I can't believe you didn't know. You're so dumb Jaya Jones.

On the way home mum asks me how it went and I pretend to be asleep so I don't have to talk about it. Then

Bee says to mum what time is her appointment tomorrow? And mum says nine thirty. Bee says have you talked to her about it? And mum says sort of. Then I get really scared because now I remember what's happening tomorrow.

the clinic

The nurse gives me a tube and says do you think you can squeeze one out for me love? I feel really embarrassed because I know she means a wee. Mum tries to come in with me, but I say I can manage by myself thanks and make her wait outside. I go into the cubicle and lock the door and look at the tube in my hand. It's clear plastic with a white sticker on it. I unscrew the lid, pull down my tights and knickers and sit on the toilet. I hold the tube under my bum in the place where I think the wee will come out. I don't feel like a wee. What am I going to tell the nurse if I can't do one? I hope she won't be cross. My wee is still not coming out. Maybe I should ask for a glass of water. Mum knocks on the door and asks if I need any help but I can't answer because the wee has started to come out and I have to move the tube around to catch it. It's very hard to wee into the tube because I can't see what I'm doing and there's only a little dribble. I wee on my hand and my sleeve but I manage to catch a little bit in the tube. There's not much in there. I hope it'll be enough. I wrap it in a paper towel because it's wet and also I don't want anyone to see it because it's embarrassing. Then I wash my hands and hold my sleeve under the dryer. Mum knocks on the door again so I unlock it and let her in. She asks me if I'm OK and I say yes even though I'm not. She looks really pale and I feel bad because I know she's worried about me. I ask her if we can go home now but she says no, they have to do a swab and a blood test next. I'm not sure what a swab is but I've had a blood test before and it was horrible. I tell her again that I'm not poorly and that I don't need any tests but I can tell she's not listening to me. She smiles and says come on Jaya, the nurse will think we've fallen down the toilet and I know she's trying to make me laugh but it doesn't work.

When the needle goes into my arm I open my mouth to tell mum the truth so that the nurse will stop. I open my mouth but the words won't come out so instead I just sit and watch the tube filling up with my blood. I think I'm going to be sick. Then the nurse asks me if I've ever had a vaginal swab before and mum says no. The nurse says she's going to insert a long cotton bud into my vagina. She says don't worry because it won't hurt but might feel a bit uncomfortable. She asks me to lie on the bed with my knees and ankles together and then tells me to let my knees flop apart. I try to do what she asks but my legs go really stiff and I can't do it. I tell her I'm too embarrassed but she just laughs and says she's seen it all before sweetheart and not to worry. Mum holds my hand and the nurse tells me too relax and think nice thoughts so I think about my favourite clothes shops. But even though I try to imagine I'm at Merry Hill, I can still feel what's happening and it's weird and horrible. Then the nurse says there you go love all finished and I ask her if we can go home now and she says yes of course. She tells me I can get dressed and pulls the curtain around the bed. Then I hear her tell mum that we'll get the results in about a week. Mum starts to cry and I feel bad because I already know the results. I know I'm not pregnant and that I haven't caught any horrible germs. I know John has a girlfriend and that she's called Sarah. I should tell mum the truth, but I can't. Instead I just keep my mouth shut and put my knickers and tights back on.

sorry

I've been so horrible to mum. When we got back from the clinic she tried to hug me, but I pushed her away and called her a fat ugly cow. I don't know why I said that to her because mum is actually very slim and pretty. I was just so angry with her for calling the police and for making me go to the horrible clinic and for believing my stupid lie in the first place. I thought she would shout back at me like she normally does when we fight but she just put her fist in her mouth and walked out the room. I don't know why she did that. It was much worse than shouting. Now I don't know what to say to her. I've never seen her like this before, not even when she broke up with Adam and Harry. She's acting so weird. I really want to make it all better, but I don't know how.

I'm sorry mum. I love you. Sometimes I hurt with the feeling of it. I love you because you are kind and beautiful and funny. I love you and would be lost without you. When I'm sad I see your face and it makes me feel better. When I'm angry I listen to your voice and it makes me feel calm. When I was young I was angry *all* the time. I couldn't say the things I wanted to say or do the things I wanted to do and it made me mad. That's why you sent me to special school. I hated special school because the teachers made us do jigsaws all day and it was really boring. Then you found out about the jigsaws and went to the school and shouted at the teachers. I was really embarrassed because you stood at the front of the class and yelled in front of everyone. Then you took my hand and said come on Jaya, you're not spending another minute in this bloody place. We walked out of the school in the middle of the day and I never went back. You sent me to another school after that, which was much better and not as boring. But it was you who taught me to read and write and speak properly. Even the teachers in my new school didn't think I ever would. Sometimes I got angry with you, but you said you would never give up on me. I remember shouting at you and calling you horrible names. I didn't mean it. It was just so hard to remember all the different letters and words and they kept getting jumbled up in my head. Once I told you that I hated you but you didn't seem to mind. You said, you don't really hate me Jaya, you're just frustrated. Afterwards I looked up the word frustrated in the dictionary and you were so proud that you nearly hugged the breath out of me. Then we sat down and had a really long talk. You said you were sorry I was so upset, but that you were trying to do what was best for me.

I know you always try to do what is best for me and I know how much you love me. I remember the worst thing that ever happened to me and how angry and sad you were. The boys on the bus were really horrible to me and I was so upset that I couldn't stop crying for ages afterwards. You cried too, after you kicked the bus-shelter. It was the first time I'd been on a bus on my own. The two boys were sitting behind me and one of them asked me for my phone number. I was proud because you'd helped me learn it off by heart and taught me how to write it down too. So I wrote it down on my bus ticket and gave it to him and he looked at it and laughed and laughed. He said you write like a five year old are you stoo-pid or what? Then he showed my bus ticket to his friend and he started to laugh too and said pretty face shame she's thick as pig shit. Then the first boy used his tongue to push out the bit of skin above his chin and he smacked the bump made by his tongue and called me a spacker. When I got off the bus you were there to meet me and as soon as I saw you I cried and cried. I told you what the boys had said and you said you were going to bloody kill them but I said they already got off the bus. That's when you kicked the bus shelter and got into trouble with that old lady who said you should know better. And you said to her it's all very well having a go at me but no-one had the guts to stand up to the yobs on the bus who were bullying my daughter. And the old lady said I would have said something if I'd seen it and you said good for you love. That was the worst day of my life even though you took me to Pizza Hut as a special treat to cheer me up. But it didn't work because the boys had made me feel bad about myself and that's why I remember it even though it was a long time ago. I remember what you said to me in Pizza Hut too. You said Jaya sometimes horrible people say horrible things and there's no rhyme or reason to it, but you are someone very special and I want you to always remember that.

You were right about horrible people saying horrible things, just like you are right about most things. I wish I could tell you the truth so you can make it all better. But, I can't. I'm scared to talk to you, mum. You pretend that everything is OK and talk to me like nothing has happened, but your voice is squeaky and your words are messy and your eyes are fluttery and frightened. I know it's my fault. I'm the one who made you sad and angry and afraid. I didn't mean to upset you. I want to make you better. I want to tell you that I lied and that I'm sorry. It didn't feel like lying because I really *really* wanted it to be true. But it wasn't. John doesn't love me and he never has. I made it all up in my head. It was all a dream, I know that now. I dreamed and dreamed of being with John and my dreams felt real. You always used to say never give up on your dreams, because sometimes dreams come true. But you were wrong. My dream didn't come true. My dream made the people I love sad and it made me sad too.

PART FOUR
IZZIE

'A mother's love for her child is like nothing else in the world. It knows no law, no pity. It dares all things and crushes down remorselessly all that stands in its path.'

Agatha Christie

the present – silence

Jaya isn't talking to me. I don't know why. Has she been traumatised by the STI clinic? Is it a delayed reaction to the rape? Post-traumatic stress disorder? A nervous breakdown? In the absence of an explanation, I resort to desperate hypothesis, while she... she stares at walls and through windows, her lovely eyes dark and expressionless. At first I tried to maintain chatty normality – offering regular cups of tea, planning future shopping trips, analysing the plot-lines of her favourite soaps. But then the sound of my spoken words began to grate on my nerves. It was if I was listening to a recording of my voice for the very first time. Every vowel, every consonant sounded loud, discordant, disjointed. My words filled the space between Jaya and I, hanging so heavily in the air that I no longer knew what to say or how to say it. So instead I tried physical means of communicating and of expressing my love; smoothing her hair, stroking her cheek, patting her arm, rubbing her shoulders... she neither repelled nor encouraged me. Bee says I should give her some space and that she'll talk to me when she's ready. I cling gratefully to this advice as I'm too emotionally exhausted to go on making small talk and pretending that everything is OK. Now I too have retreated, guiltily, thankfully, into a world of silence. But without words to bind us together, I am a stranger to my daughter and she to me. Without words to tether me to the present, I feel aimless and disconnected. Without words to distract me, my guilt intensifies and takes over. Without words I am lost.

And so it is that tonight I lie awake in my mute fortress, listening to the silence and loathing it. Everything is quiet. Everything, that is, except for my conscience, which berates me with thunderous clarity. Every thought in my head is loud, merciless and unbearable. I jump from my bed and walk over to the mirror on my bedroom wall. In the moonlight my face is pale and ghostly. When I was at school there was a crack in one of the mirrors in the girls' toilets. Legend had it that if you stared into that mirror and chanted three times, 'Victoria, Victoria, show me your face', the face of a murdered schoolgirl would appear alongside your reflection. All us girls tried it and I doubt any of us ever beheld anything but our own freckled features. I do remember though staring into that mirror with all the intensity and earnestness of youth and becoming utterly captivated by my own mirror image. It wasn't vanity or self-obsession which so entranced me, but rather the realisation that gazing upon my reflection for a long period of time rendered it meaningless. I try this again now and experience the same dizzying sense of detachment, as if there is absolutely nothing connecting me to the image I see in the mirror. As a child I found this sensation fascinating, but right now, in my soundless prison, it is more than I can physically cope with. I start to scream, beating my breast like a mountain gorilla. It does me good. The awful silence is broken, my chest throbs with life-affirming pain and relief washes over me. Panting and breathless, I suddenly remember Jaya. Have I disturbed her? I creep into her room. She is sleeping so peacefully, it breaks my heart. I get into bed next to her, enfold her in my arms and, as the sleep I so crave continues to elude me, I allow my mind to wander...

the past – time

My love of solitude was born on a windswept beach at dusk. I was eleven years old and on holiday with my parents on the Welsh coast. It was out of season, cold and blowy, but I don't think I've ever been so happy. For two weeks I roamed the surrounding hills and beaches all alone, returning to the B&B in the evening with tight, tingling skin and a crazy hairstyle. For me, freedom will always taste of wintry sea spray and a mouthful of hair. On the last evening of the holiday, two things happened which I will never forget. That afternoon, I walked five miles along the seashore to a coastal caravan park. Where the park bordered the beach, a line of old railway sleepers had been erected to protect the caravans from the wild Atlantic waters. During the holiday, I had spent many contented hours perched on top of those sleepers and I had a romantic notion that it would be the perfect spot from which to watch the sunset and bid farewell to the ocean. As I sat in rapturous admiration, watching the sun melt into the frothy sea, I felt an unexpected unfurling, burgeoning sensation between my thighs. It would be inaccurate to describe the feeling as sexual, it was more like an intense yearning, but it was at that precise moment, in that wonderful location that I first became aware of a new and unknown part of my body. It was an unforgettable moment.

It was immediately followed by a second, equally memorable occurrence. All my young life I had been filled with longing for something indefinable and unobtainable and it left me feeling aimless and rootless. But as I sat there, my senses heightened, my need for beauty satiated, I was suddenly overcome by a powerful feeling of contentment. For the first time in my life, I felt *connected*, both to myself and to the physical world. It was such a blissful experience that I wanted to remain in that moment forever and so, with both hands, I grasped the wooden sleepers on either side of me. I held on for dear life, as if clutching something physical and immovable would somehow pin me forever into that moment in time. And for a split second, I truly believed that, with the sheer strength of my grip, I could exert my will on the universe. When I eventually let go, my hands were locked into a painful claw-like shape and there was a big splinter in one of my fingers. Since that day, I've often repeated this strange ritual at happy moments in my life, but I've never again experienced the overwhelming emotion of that first time.

Five years later, at the tender age of sixteen, I fell in love. He was much older, our parish priest no less and, although he could never bring himself to "consummate" our relationship, he made impassioned and poetic declarations of love, which captured and inflamed my young heart. We had deep theological discussions about God and love, trying to convince ourselves that He would want his servants to be happy together and that He had designed man and woman for this purpose. My priest promised to leave the church for me, but in the end he couldn't face the fury of the bishop, or the disgust of his parishioners, or whatever, and so one day he missed our regular rendezvous at the church and every other one after that and I... I was utterly heartbroken. Having been abandoned at the altar, so to speak, I experienced the exact polar opposite emotion to that which I had felt that evening on the beach; I lay on my bed, gripped my pillow and *willed* myself into the future, desperate to be transported to a time and place where the pain and suffering of the present would be less.

Although I've often tried, therefore, I've sadly never managed to manipulate space and time to my advantage. But perhaps I've never wished quite hard enough. Tonight I know I am. I wish I could stay in this moment for all time, with my arms wrapped around my slumbering child. I wish we could float off the bed, out of the window and land five years ago, when Jaya was safe and there was still time to protect her from the monster who hurt her. I wish I could fly around the planet and send it spinning backward on its axis the way Superman did to save Lois. I wish, *I wish*, I WISH. But I know that, in one hour dawn will break, in three, Jaya will awake, in four we'll have our breakfast together and life will continue at the same pace it always has. Time will not pause, fast-forward, or rewind; all I can hope is that someday it will heal.

adam

I did learn to love again after my priest. Only once. His name was Adam.

Ten years ago in January, Bee and I made a new year's resolution. We called it "Operation Get a Life", the irony of which made us giggle as we sat sipping lemonade in the pub. Although somewhat anticlimactic and involving only a very occasional night out, it still felt delightfully illicit. On those nights, we roped Bee's sister into looking after the kids and fled our homes like naughty children playing truant from school. Our favourite haunt was Ma Pardoe's on Halesowen Road, a delightful old pub, full of Black Country charm and colourful characters. Famous for its home-brewed ales and traditional features, the pub was always full to the rafters and we loved the atmosphere, which was homely yet vibrant. One evening in Ma Pardoe's, I met Adam. He was a dentist from Stourbridge and I was instantly attracted to him. He was green-eyed and slim-hipped, with full lips which he could magically transform into either a beautiful pout or an aphrodisiac smile. He had the impertinent charm of the self-consciously good-looking, which made me want to both smack him and sleep with him in equal measure. I remember our first ever conversation.

'Is anyone sitting there?' he asked me, nodding towards the empty chair opposite mine.

'Yeah, my friend's in the toilet,' I replied.

'I'm sure she won't mind when she sees you're chatting to me,' he said, lowering himself into Bee's chair. I mentally slapped and then undressed him.

I wasn't looking for any kind of relationship, least of all a serious one; Jaya was going through a particularly difficult period and the last thing she needed in her life was a new boyfriend in mine. But these things are impossible to plan and rarely convenient. Although I had always tried to put her first, I just couldn't give Adam up. My feelings for him were messy, illogical and glorious; he got under my skin and turned me inside out. For Jaya's sake though, I insisted we take things slowly, which of course had the exact opposite effect on him. Adam seemed to think I was playing "hard to get" and my apparent deliberation only made him keener. When he eventually realised that it wasn't a game and that I really was serious about protecting my daughter's feelings, it was too late for the poor man; he was totally and utterly smitten.

Adam had never been married, but had not long come out of a twelve year relationship. I therefore assumed that he was just not the marrying type, which didn't bother me in the slightest. He and Jaya got along fine, which was a huge relief to me. He made her laugh with his childish antics and his huge repertoire of comic voices. He told me that he found her sweet and fun, although I could tell that, at times, he was jealous of the close bond we shared and was frustrated that I would always put her feelings before his. This caused a few nasty arguments, which were always pointless because nothing he could ever say or do would alter the fact that Jaya was my top priority. The worst of these arguments happened about a year into our relationship. He booked a romantic getaway to Thailand and surprised me with it. He'd thought of every little detail; he'd asked Bee to look after Jaya for the week, he'd bought me a whole new wardrobe of summer clothes *and* packed them in a brand new suitcase, he'd found my passport in my desk drawer, he'd booked a limo to take us to the airport – every was perfect. Except... he had forgotten that Jaya had an important hospital appointment that week, which we'd been waiting six months for. She'd been having "absences", not quite seizures, but strange episodes when she would become unresponsive and stare into space. I was really worried about her and the GP had suggested it could be some kind of epilepsy. And so, when Adam sprung his surprise on me, producing our passports with a theatrical flourish, all I felt was anger at his thoughtlessness. I told him flatly that I couldn't go to Ko Samui with him, which didn't go down particularly well.

'What the hell do you mean you can't go?'

I regarded him coldly. 'I mean,' I began, speaking slowly and deliberately, adding insult to injury, 'I... can't... go.'

He stared at me in disbelief, his mouth opening and closing like an indignant halibut. 'But it's all arranged!' he ranted. 'We leave tonight!'

'Well take someone else, because I won't be going with you.'

'I don't want to take anyone buggering else!' he exploded. 'I want to take my girlfriend.'

'Well, I'm very sorry that my daughter's brain scan messes up your holiday plans, but I'm afraid it's rather more important to me than frolicking on a beach in a bloody bikini!'

He smacked his head, remembering, feeling guilty.

'Oh God, Iz, I'm so sorry.'

I nodded, curtly, not trusting myself to speak. He took my hand.

'I just spotted this amazing deal in the travel agent and got carried away. I'm an unthinking idiot. Forgive me.' I nodded again, more warmly this time; but just as I was prepared to be conciliatory, he sighed and shook his head.

'I just can't help feeling that if it hadn't been this, it would have been something else.'

My hackles went straight back up. 'What do you mean?' I growled.

'I don't know. I suppose what I mean is that there's always going to be something getting in the way of us being together'. He looked at me sadly. 'We can't go on like this.'

'Oh, OK,' I said, preparing myself for the inevitable break-up speech. 'So, what are you saying?'

'Marry me.'

To say I was surprised is an understatement. But the look on Adam's face was of pure amazement, as if a ventriloquist had just run into the room, proposed marriage on his behalf and run out again.

'Are you serious?' I asked him.

He took a few seconds to consider the question and then began to laugh in delight and wonderment.

'Oh God, I *am*,' he giggled, 'I really, really am!'

'So, let's just get this straight. You're asking me—'

He interrupted me by flinging himself to the floor and skidding towards me on one knee.

'Isabel Jones, will you do me the extreme honour of being my wife?'

The next three months were the happiest of my life. Jaya was over the moon at the prospect of being a bridesmaid, Bee and I had lots of fun planning the wedding and Adam was so overjoyed that he had a great big silly grin permanently plastered across his face. We were so in love that it must have been vomit-inducing to other people. I mentioned this to Adam and it riled him.

'For crying out loud, Iz! You've had so little happiness in your life, can't you just be happy to be happy?'

Happy to be happy! That made me smile.

'Adam?' I asked him with mock seriousness. 'Should I be happy that I'm happy that I'm happy?' He kissed the top of my head.

'Just be happy that I love you and you love me,' he said.

Plagued by self-doubt as I am, I sometimes found this simple reality hard to accept. 'Why do you love me, Adam?' was a question I often asked. 'I just do,' he would always reply. And that should have been that... but unfortunately it wasn't. Because it wasn't enough that he loved me, he had to love Jaya too.

A few weeks before the wedding, he ran into my kitchen, excitedly waving a rolled-up newspaper in the air.

'I've found a great house for us,' he said, spinning me away from the cooker and dancing me around the table. 'It has three big bedrooms, so I could have a study and you can have that gym you've always dreamed of.'

For a split second, I allowed myself to be carried along on the wave of his enthusiasm, until I realised exactly what he had just said.

'And what about Jaya?' I asked. 'Where will she sleep?'

He looked uncomfortable. 'Yeah, of course one of the rooms will be for Jaya,' he said. 'I was just thinking that, in an ideal world, we—'

'What?' I interrupted, furiously. 'In an ideal world we'd live on our own?'

'No,' he said firmly, 'in an ideal world, we'd have a study and a gym.'

'Well, that doesn't sound like *my* ideal world, Adam.'

'OK, OK,' he said, holding up his hands to fend off my wrath.

'In my ideal world,' I continued, 'I'd live with my daughter.'

'Of course—'

'Forever.'

He looked appalled at this. 'Forever?' he asked in a small voice. 'What? Like for the rest of your life?'

'Forever, Adam.' I couldn't believe we were having this conversation at this point in our relationship. 'What did you expect? In case it's escaped your notice, she's got a learning disability!'

He looked genuinely baffled. 'But that doesn't mean she won't want her independence one day.'

'What the fuck does that mean?' I felt dizzy with rage and grief. 'You'd want to put her in some bloody care home?'

'No. I don't know. Some sort of supported living, maybe?'

I shrugged off his suggestion with the contempt it deserved, but Adam was unapologetic.

'Well I'm sure *she* won't want to be tied to your apron strings for the rest of her life.'

'And are you thinking about what's best for her or what's best for you?' I demanded.

Adam hesitated for a split second, which was a split second too long. When he looked into my eyes, he had composed himself again. 'Isabel,' he said, 'I love you and I want to be with you for the rest of my life. And if that means taking on Jaya, then that's a price I'm willing to pay.' He smiled, satisfied that he had placated me.

'*The price you're willing to pay?*' I repeated through gritted teeth. He grabbed me by the arms, shaking his head, realising the damage his words had caused.

'No, no, no Isabel, please.'

But it was too late. 'So that's all Jaya is to you, is it? The downside to an otherwise good relationship?'

'You know that's not what I meant. Please, baby, we can work this out.'

But he was wrong. We couldn't and we never did. Although he did try once, about six months later. The ironic thing is that, as it turns out, he was right about Jaya. She did want her independence from me in the end. Sadly though, her bid for freedom has cost us both dear.

harry

After Adam and I split up, I had some sort of nervous episode – possibly a breakdown, although I never had this medically confirmed. Bee says that, at the time, she thought I'd actually eloped with Adam and left a clone in my place; a decoy Isabel who looked and sounded exactly like me, but wasn't me. It was a dark and frightening time in my life. I felt lonely, anxious and unable to make even the most basic of decisions. I worried that the authorities would find out and Jaya would be taken away from me. I was constantly gasping for breath and it got to the point when I could no longer go out alone for fear of hyperventilating. Sometimes these panic attacks would creep into my dreams, sending sweat pumping through my pores and adrenaline through my veins. I would awake, sodden and shaking, feeling my broken heart twitch through my nightdress. In short, I wasn't very well.

I decided that I could no longer cope on my own and that I needed to find another man. It was a drastic step. I'd been single for most of my adult life and had always been, if not exactly happy, then at least self-sufficient and autonomous. Of course, I'd loved being with Adam, but never felt as if I couldn't manage without him. Still, I was convinced that it was the only possible solution and so placed an ad in the lonely hearts section of the local paper. I still have the cutting to remind myself of what a deluded fool I was and as a warning never to do it again.

Lonely single mum, looking for that special someone. Attractive, late-twenties, GSOH, WLTM similar for fun and possible romance.

'It's too soon,' warned Bee.

'You're wrong,' I assured her, 'I'm ready for a real, adult relationship, now. Adam has opened my eyes. I can't do celibacy any more.' But Bee remained grim-faced and unconvinced.

'Isabel, listen to me. You're still in love with your ex-fiancé, three months ago you were planning your wedding. This is not a good idea.'

Wise words from my wise friend. I would have saved myself much suffering in life had I always heeded her advice.

After a few weeks of dating various inappropriate, over-zealous and/or badly-behaved men, I arranged to meet up with Harry. Although my memory of him is now distorted by what was to come, I think I must have liked him at first. I know that he didn't make my heart race in the way that Adam had, but he did make me smile. Everything about Harry was broad; his chest, his smile, his waistline, his Black Country accent. On our very first date, he wrapped me up in a big bear hug and lifted me clean off the ground.

'You'm the best looking wench I've ever clapped eyes on!' he proclaimed.

In my emotionally weakened state, I found his "larger-than-life" persona appealing, although for the life of me, I don't know how I ended up becoming his girlfriend. It was probably just vanity on my part; he seemed to find me utterly irresistible and no girl can resist being irresistible.

He put me on a pedestal and I suppose I was just happy to perch there for a while, however precariously. After a couple of months though, I felt that my tenure as Sex Goddess was coming to an end. Being with Harry was beginning to feel strange and somehow wrong; intimate moments were starting to feel sordid, conversations were becoming strained, enjoyable nights out were turning into endurance tests. To be fair on Harry, it wasn't his fault. Bee had been right of course, I wasn't ready for a new relationship. I had stupidly thought that throwing myself at another man would help me get over Adam, but instead it only made me miss him all the more. I vowed to let Harry down gently at the next available opportunity.

That was my intention, anyway; but then something happened which made me postpone my break-up with Harry. That something, as always, was Jaya. Her tenth birthday was fast approaching and I'd promised her a big party to make up for the frequent hospital trips and all the poking and prodding she'd endured. Unfortunately, we were no closer to discovering what was causing the strange lapses in consciousness, but I was thankful at least that the brain scan had ruled out epilepsy. Then, a couple of weeks before her birthday, a kindly doctor took me to one side and asked me if he could be "frank".

'Of course,' I told him, 'I want your honest opinion.'

'The thing is,' he said, 'I think these episodes may well be stress-related.'

'You mean there's nothing actually wrong with her?' I asked.

'I'm not saying that,' he replied, 'stress can be a serious condition. If anxiety is the cause, then you should take it very seriously.' He gave me a paternal smile. 'Is there anything you can think of which might be worrying Jaya at present?'

'At present?' I thought about my recent break-up with Adam and subsequent meltdown. I thought about Jaya's troubled little face whenever she found me crying into my cornflakes or dithering over which pair of socks she should wear. I thought about my swift change of partner and what a traumatic experience this must have been for her. 'At present?' I repeated. 'Only everything.'

After that, I decided that it really wasn't the right time to end things with Harry. If Jaya was indeed suffering from stress then the last thing she needed was more upheaval in her life, especially when she was so looking forward to her birthday party. The other thing to consider was that she really seemed to like Harry and always perked up whenever he was around. So, with breath-taking cowardice and selfishness, I decided to stay with him, for the short term at least. I'm not proud of what I did and I was sufficiently ashamed at the time to confess all to Bee. She wasn't impressed to say the least.

'So, let me get this straight. For the sake of your daughter, you broke up with a man you loved and now, because of her, you're staying with a man you don't? You have to admit Iz, that's rather odd behaviour.'

'Well yes, when you look at it like that.'

'And is there any other way to look at it?' she asked me, bluntly. I had to admit, she had me there.

Despite Bee's protests, I invited Harry to Jaya's birthday party and spent the day trying to be the perfect hostess, mother and girlfriend, whilst all the time despising myself.

As the party wound down and Jaya was sitting in the lounge listening to music with her friends, there was a knock on the front door. Bee and I were clearing up in the kitchen and I was up to my elbows in soapy water, so Harry gallantly offered to put down his paper and answer it.

'It's probably Anne from next door,' I told Bee, 'she said she might pop in after bingo.' But Bee was looking past me into the hallway.

'It's not Anne from next door,' she said, quietly. I followed her gaze and saw Harry leading Adam down the narrow corridor towards us.

'Oh shit,' I said.

Harry strode purposefully into the kitchen and stood beside me, putting a proprietorial arm around my shoulder. Adam followed, his face thunderous, his hands behind his back.

'Says he's a friend of yours, babe,' said Harry. I nodded, red-faced and silent.

Then, because my speechlessness was becoming deeply embarrassing, Bee introduced the two men with a curt, 'Harry, Adam, Adam, Harry.'

They eyed each other suspiciously, until Adam suddenly broke the silence: 'Well, you didn't waste any fucking time did you?'

'Adam, please,' I begged.

He produced two bouquets of red roses from behind his back, flung them at me and turned on his heel.

'And to think I've been crying over *you*,' he spat, as he walked out the door. I chased him down the hallway, past a worried looking Jaya in the doorway of the lounge and out into the street. He was already in his car, revving the engine, loudly.

'ADAM!' I shrieked, throwing myself onto the bonnet in dramatic fashion. He switched off the engine and wound down the window.

'Get off my car, Izzie.'

'Adam, please don't go,' I pleaded, hot tears streaming down my face. I walked round to the open window and put my head inside his car. 'Please stay.'

'What for?' he demanded. 'So you, me and lover-boy in there can have a cosy night in together?'

'I love you.'

He shook his head sadly. 'I love you too,' he said. 'I came here today to wish Jaya a happy birthday and to tell you just how important you both are...,' he checked himself, '...*were* to me.'

'Please, baby, we can work this out,' I said, echoing the very words he had said to me only a few months previously. He looked at me in that way of his, his eyes wet and shining with love, and I felt a surge of hope.

'Please tell me you haven't slept with *that* man,' he implored. The look on my face must have given me away, because he choked back a cry, turned the key in the ignition and revved up the engine again.

'I couldn't even *look* at another woman so soon after you,' he said before winding up the window and driving out of my life forever.

I returned to the house, grief-stricken yet resolute. Inside, Bee had discreetly joined the girls in the lounge. The music had been turned up and I could hear laughter from within. Harry was waiting for me at the kitchen table. He stood when I walked in, taking in my tear-stained face and dishevelled appearance.

'Everything OK?' he asked.

'Not really,' I replied. 'Look Harry, I'm sorry to have to do this now, but—'

He held up his hand to silence me. 'Don't say it!'

'Harry please, things really aren't working out between —'

But once more I didn't get to finish my sentence, because I suddenly found myself flying across the room, having been knocked off my feet by a powerful backhander. When I eventually managed to focus my eyes, Harry's meaty paw was still raised above his head and his square chin was jutting out in righteous indignation.

'I'm sorry it had to come to that, Isabel,' he told me, as if striking me across the face had been an unfortunate, yet unavoidable consequence of my own actions. Then he held out his hand to me to help me up.

'You must be joking,' I said hoarsely, rejecting the proffered hand.

'It's alright, bab,' he said, 'I don't hold no grudges. Take my hand and we'll say no more about it.'

Unbelievable!

'Harry, you total fucking bastard,' I shrieked, springing to my feet, energised by the combined force of my rage and grief. 'Get the fuck out of my house! I NEVER want to see you again!' I squared up to him, bracing myself for another punch in the face, but it never came. Instead, I watched in horror as Harry's solid, manly features crumpled and he began to cry. At that moment, Bee flew into the kitchen like a wild thing.

'What *on earth* is going on in here?' she demanded. I jabbed a finger at Harry.

'He—' Jab. 'Hit—' Jab, jab. 'Me!'

'But I love you,' he whimpered in protest.

Bee could not have looked more stunned if she'd walked into the kitchen and discovered a portal to a parallel universe. Harry began to wail loudly.

'Oh my life, Harry, pull yourself together!' roared Bee. 'Are you a man or a mouse?!'

Harry, like many perpetrators of domestic violence, was in fact a mouse and left with his tail between his legs. Only then did I allow myself to succumb to the wave of hysteria which had been mounting since Adam walked into the kitchen. Bee tells me I became a quivering, jabbering wreck, although I don't remember a thing. She put me to bed, calmed Jaya's terrified guests and saw them off with a placatory word to their parents. It wasn't my finest moment but at least, thanks to Harry, I got my fighting spirit back and found the strength to carry on without Adam. Adam. That special someone. I try not to think about him now. Too many painful memories.

a bad memory

We forget so much of what happens to us in our lifetimes, and yet sometimes the seemingly most bizarre and obscure detail can stay lodged in our minds forever. Plenty of sad, bad and mad things have happened to me in my life, but my worst memory, the one that still makes me feel panicky and nauseous when I think of it, is a pair of tiny feet sticking out of a child's play tent.

Like many conscientious stay-at-home mums, I took my toddler to a playgroup to stimulate her social and mental development. Being naturally reticent, I didn't mix well with the other mothers and I found it almost impossible to cope with their reactions towards Jaya. As a tiny tot she was angelically beautiful, which was a curse rather than a blessing for the poor kid. I noticed that most of the mothers had the same reaction when they first met Jaya. Initially they would gravitate towards her, cooing and crowing, but their words of praise and admiration soon died on their lips when they heard the animalistic grunts and squawks which, back then, were her only means of communication. She frightened both the other children in the group and their well-meaning mums, who would continually nag and encourage them to include Jaya in their games. Her erratic behaviour and lack of speech were so at odds with the loveliness of her appearance, that people were at a genuine loss as to how to approach her. I truly believe that had she been less attractive, or more obviously "disabled", then other children and adults would have been more tolerant and understanding of her. As it was, by the end of the third session, I was ready to give up. Then, an amazing thing happened; Jaya began to play with another child. The little girl was younger than her, but was lively and gregarious. At first, I observed their tentative interactions like a hawk watching over her young, but after a few weeks, I began to relax and even chatted with the other mums as they played.

There was one woman there with whom I got on particularly well. Her name was Theresa and we found we had a lot in common. She was also from a staunchly Catholic family and had caused a huge scandal by having an illegitimate child. Unlike me however, she was now married and respectable, her parents and the father of her child having stuck by her and, between them, struck up a bargain to rescue her honour. Theresa felt she had been lucky, although from what she told me of her roving, alcoholic husband, he was no great prize. Still, she was sufficiently happy with her own life so as to regard mine with lip-trembling sympathy. If I'm honest, I really did like Theresa and I began to look forward to my weekly therapy sessions when I would pour out my sorrows to her, while she nodded, tutted, patted my hand and dabbed at her eyes with Kleenex.

Jaya's friendship with the little girl had made her more socially acceptable to the other tots and every week she was included in more and more of their games. Full of maternal pride, I would watch her as she gambolled around with her new friends. No matter how deep in discussion I was with Theresa, I would keep an eye on Jaya and was always acutely aware of where she was in the room. One day, a new play-tent was erected in a corner of the room. It was a real hit with the kids, especially with Jaya, who crawled inside at the very beginning of the session and then refused to come out again. Although I couldn't see her, I could hear her giggling and babbling contentedly to herself and so I left her to it. I noticed several more children going into the tent and was aware that it was becoming a hub of increasingly wild activity, but didn't think much of it until suddenly I realised that I could no longer distinguish Jaya's voice above the general racket. I looked towards the tent and what I saw was so incongruously horrific that it has been forever scorched into my memory. The imprints of little hands, heads and elbows caused the tent to bulge and stretch in such a manner that it resembled an animal carcass, its taut skin teeming with maggots. The front flaps lolled open and sticking out of these were Jaya's feet; tiny, vulnerable, unmoving. Time stopped. Theresa's mouth moved but no sound issued forth. I jumped to my feet in slow motion. Ripping open the tent-flaps, I saw Jaya lying motionless on the floor, staring up at about five or six other children as they poked, prodded, shook and slapped her. It wasn't a vicious beating, more like the curious baiting of an injured animal; but Jaya's reaction, her passive acceptance of such aggression, aroused within me a white hot fury.

'Get away from her!' I bellowed, as I gathered Jaya in my arms. Within a heartbeat, a dozen hostile mothers surrounded me. June, the woman who ran the group, put a warning hand on my shoulder.

'Isabel, *please...*'

I shrugged her off and pointed at the bemused children still in the tent. 'They were physically assaulting my daughter!' I yelled. One of them began to cry.

'Y... you're frightening the ch... children,' stammered June, her eyes wide with emotion.

It snapped me out of my rage. I looked around at the horrified faces of the other mothers, most of whom were shielding their kids from me as if I were an axe-wielding maniac. The mother of the crying boy snatched him up and turned on me.

'For goodness sake,' she shouted, 'they were probably just playing.'

I shook my head. 'No, it wasn't a game. They were hurting her.'

The woman rolled her eyes. Of course, she wasn't going to believe me. It was her child I was accusing. She cradled her sobbing son, her lips resting on the top of his head.

'Anyway, your kid's a lunatic,' she mumbled into his hair. At first I thought I'd heard wrong.

'*What?* What did you just say?!' I demanded.

The woman shrugged. 'Well it's true,' she said. 'All that screeching and grunting. It's not normal. My little lad's scared to death of her.'

I would probably have throttled her had June not stepped in again.

'Look, Isabel,' she began, 'perhaps this isn't the right environment for Jaya, after all. It would probably be best for everyone if you found a... a more *appropriate* group.'

It was my first real glimpse of the bullying and discrimination which Jaya would often come across in later life. Sadly, I have since become accustomed to such ignorance and prejudice, but that first time it *hurt*.

As we left, I tried to make eye contact with Theresa, but she studiously avoided my gaze. My first real attempt at friendship had spectacularly failed. I had opened up my heart to Theresa, but after that day I slammed it back shut, locked it, chained it and threw away the key. Three years later, on a windy playground in September, poor Bee suffered the consequences. It often amazes me that she ever bothered to try to get to know me better, but she did, and I'm eternally grateful.

a very special friendship

Bee's story is an unhappy one. Coerced into an arranged marriage at just eighteen, she fell almost instantly pregnant. In his first weeks and months on earth, baby Kishan experienced more pain and suffering than most people do in a lifetime. Born eight weeks prematurely, he spent the first two months of his life in hospital with wires and tubes piercing his soft new skin. He had his first epileptic seizure at just three days old and a few days later his little heart stopped and had to be restarted. When his parents eventually got him home, it soon became apparent that Kishan's epilepsy was just the tip of the iceberg and that he would need round the clock support and care for the rest of his life. It was more than their already fragile relationship could withstand and, two years after he set off for his new life in England, Bina's husband returned to Gujarat a broken and exhausted man. Bee never blamed him.

'He was a nice man,' she once told me, 'just not very strong. Under different circumstances, I think we could have been happy together.'

I know that I have a tendency towards self-pity, but I'm also aware that I have a lot to be grateful for. When I think of Bee's life, I feel humble and contrite; it's been so much more difficult than mine. On the face of it, fate has dealt us startlingly similar cards: both single mothers to a child with a disability, both fairly intelligent, attractive, independent, strong-minded, broke, lonely. All the same, I feel sorry for her and, although I'd never dare say it to her face, I feel sorry for her because of Kishan. I just don't know how she copes; loving and caring for him the way she does, without any hint that he loves and cares for her in return. No hugs, no reciprocated smiles, no shared jokes or interests; she'll never know what it feels like to have her son throw his arms around her and say, 'I love you, mum.' Although she maintains that he does communicate with her in his own way, I've never seen any real evidence of it and think it's just wishful thinking on her part. She's convinced that he's "in there somewhere", an "inner" Kishan, unable to communicate with the outside world, yet rational and coherent in his thought. In fact, she's so certain of his hidden abilities, that she spends hours with him every week, reading to him, going through the alphabet, showing him spellings, punctuation and mathematical problems. Impressed as I am by her conviction and perseverance, I remain dubious. The only time I've ever heard Kishan laugh was when he was mimicking Sid James whilst watching a *Carry On* film and the sound of it was so *exactly* like the actor's lewd cackle, that I found it strangely chilling. Bee says that Kishan often makes her laugh, which is true, but it always seems to be an "if-I-don't-laugh-I'll-cry" or a "laughing-in-the-face-of-adversity" sort of laugh, rather than a spontaneous outburst of mirth. As far as I can tell, being Kishan's mum is a thankless, exhausting, relentless task and I think my friend is the bravest woman on the planet for undertaking it alone. Yet Bee adores her son and is fiercely protective of him. Kishan has been the subject of many bitter disagreements between herself and her parents.

'I've tried so many times to explain his condition to them, but they just don't get it,' she once told me. 'When he was little, my mum was always telling him off for not listening to her and dad would shout at him when he rocked back and forth. They thought his behaviour was caused by poor parenting and kept nagging me to discipline him.' The thought of anyone ever trying to discipline Kishan made me smile.

'It's not funny, Iz,' said Bee, mournfully, 'even now they view his disability as a personal failing on my part.'

'Bee, you're the best mum in the world,' I reassured her, 'never let anyone ever tell you otherwise.'

One Saturday night, not long after the infamous birthday party, my best friend and I kissed. I'm not sure who kissed who first, or who kissed who back – we were both horribly drunk – but I do remember that it was the sweetest, most sensual embrace that I'd ever known. We'd been watching a video, stretched out on Bee's living-room floor. Kishan was in respite care for the weekend and Jaya was at a schoolfriend's sleepover, so we took full advantage and bought a pizza and a bottle of wine. Within the hour, I was at the corner shop buying a second bottle, which seemed like a good idea at the time. It wasn't. Neither of us are particularly seasoned drinkers and we were soon lurching around the room to Bee's favourite Wham album, giggling and holding onto each other for mutual support. Bee slipped on the takeaway pizza box and we both toppled over onto the sofa. One thing led to another etc. etc. and the next thing I knew we were kissing. I went home straight after, too drunk to feel embarrassed but sober enough to realise that I'd be mortified the next day.

The following morning, I awoke shivering with fear. I was afraid that the kiss would change everything; that things would be strained and awkward between us, or

175

worse, that she'd never want to see me again. The thought of losing Bee made me feel physically sick. I realised then just how much I loved her, although the exact nature of my feelings had been blurred by the kiss. Uncertainty made me a coward and I ignored the ringing phone all day, only mustering the courage to ring her the following evening.

'Thought you'd emigrated,' she sniffed.

'Oh God, Bee – I'm so *so* sorry.'

'Why?' She sounded amused. 'What have you done that's so terrible? Apart from ignoring my calls, that is.'

'We kissed,' I mumbled, trailing off.

'Yes, I remember, I *was* there, you know.'

'I feel terrible.'

'Because we kissed?' She sounded genuinely bemused. 'What's the big deal? A part of your anatomy made contact with a part of my anatomy. It was nice, but it's over. Forget about it.'

I was relieved she felt that way, but for a while the kiss still bothered me. What did it mean? Was I gay? Was Bee? Was I in love with her? In the end, having no-one else to talk to, I put these questions to her. I'll never forget her answer; she looked at me gravely, put her hands on mine and said:

'Izzie, with the sole exception of my son, I love you more than anyone. And I think you love me too.' Her voice faltered and she paused, awaiting confirmation. I could barely breathe, let alone speak, but I managed to incline my head a fraction. It was enough to reassure her and she continued.

'Well, for my part, I love you just about as much and as deeply as one person can love another, and I don't want to spoil things by dissecting and categorising our feelings. Who says there has to be a *thousand* different types and classifications of love? Do you get what I'm saying?'

'Ye-es,' I replied. But still I needed some kind of answer. 'So where do we go from here?' She held up her hand to silence me.

'Izzie, just this once, let's not talk about it. Let's not question or analyse or *theorise*. We'll never get anywhere and it'll only confuse things more. So, let's just accept our relationship for what it is, eh?'

'Which is?' A huge smile lit up her face and she grabbed me in a big bear hug.

'A very special friendship, of course!'

control

Bee has been a guiding, shining light in my life. Sometimes I wonder where I'd be without her. Struggling, no doubt. Deploying all my obsessive compulsive rituals to excess; dieting, tidying-up, straightening food packets in the cupboard and exercising manically, in a vain attempt to exert control over my life. Not that I cope wonderfully well now, but at least I'm not the wiry, neurotic Isabel of the mid 90s; the Isabel who once prompted two giggling teenage mums to call me "Sarah Connor".

I was sitting in the Health Centre reception area, cradling six-week-old Jaya and minding my own business, when I noticed two young women nudging each other, whispering and staring indiscreetly in my direction. In no mood to be the butt of their silly jokes, I instantly confronted them.

'Got a problem?' I growled. I must have been pretty scary-looking, because they both shut up instantly and stared at me wide-eyed.

'Erm, no. No disrespect, like,' stammered one of the girls, 'it's just you look like someone off a film we saw the other night.'

'What film?' I asked, suspiciously. The girl who had answered me the first time elbowed the second girl in the

178

ribs, indicating that it was now her turn to communicate with the psychopath.

'*Terminator 2*,' she blurted out. I was on the point of being hugely offended (wasn't that the film with Arnold Schwarzenegger as a killer cyborg!?) when she quickly added, 'Sarah Connor.'

As I hadn't seen the film, I merely shrugged, but was relieved that they were at least comparing me to a female human character. Not long after, mildly intrigued by their comments, I rented *Terminator 2* and I too was surprised by the physical similarities between myself and Linda Hamilton's mentally unstable warrior-woman. But more than that, I felt I could relate to the character; ferocious, obsessive and ruthlessly maternal, she struck a real chord with me. I was particularly affected by the scene which shows her doing chin-ups in the psychiatric hospital. At the time, I too felt imprisoned and my daily exercise regime was just as punishing. Although there were no physical barriers to my freedom, I no longer felt in command of my life and my body was the only thing I still fully owned and dominated. Star jumps, stomach-crunches, leg-curls, skipping, sit-ups, press-ups, pull-ups; whenever my baby slept, I worked out. Such rigorous exercise so soon after giving birth was frowned upon by my health visitor, who thought I was some sort of muscled mental-case. But in reality, it was the only thing which kept me sane; it cleared the clutter, it quietened the whooshing, it stilled the swirling of a million angry thoughts. Even now, my body is living proof of my obsessive and controlling nature. My stomach muscles, biceps, calves, hips and bottom are all things which I regularly sculpt and bend to my will. Over the years, my muscle expansion has been directly proportional to my stress levels and with every worry and minor defeat, I renew the vigour of my nightly regime. I suppose it's because, still now, I don't have any real influence over anything in life.

I lost control of my life when I got pregnant and then, after Jaya was born, I lost my future too. I shelved my aspirations, because I realised that walking around with your head in the clouds, dreaming of foreign travel and spiritual enlightenment and men and sex, just wasn't conducive to raising a child with learning difficulties. I've every reason to be proud of myself. It was the responsible choice, the right decision and I've since led a solid, worthwhile existence raising and nurturing my daughter. The fact that she's grown up to become a strong-minded, confident young woman is credit to all my hard work and perseverance. But I've paid a high price. With little else to occupy my mind but Jaya, I've channelled all my energy into fighting her corner. Her life, well-being, happiness, money, housing, health, education, benefits; these are the subjects of my daily battles and power struggles. And, over the years, it's taken its toll on me. My confidence is gone; stamped out by the bureaucrats, swallowed up by the benefits system, worried away by the education, council, health and social workers. I blame the education system. I blame the local council. I blame the government.

I'm not to blame. I've tried. I've fought. I wanted to shape my own destiny, to develop my mind, to broaden my horizons. But I didn't have the energy for us both and so, naturally, I chose Jaya. I'm *not* a failure.

A SAD, PATHETIC FAILURE.

I am. I know I am. My only success in life is my beautiful girl and now I've failed her too. I can't crunch and curl it all better. No amount of physical exertion will change what has happened to Jaya; I've failed her and now I've probably lost her too.

But... didn't I fail her long before this? What kind of a role model have I been for her? A depressive, lonely mother who's built a life around organising and controlling her. Is that how she sees me? Is that why she won't talk to me? Because, really, what am I without Jaya to manage and dominate? She's my ultimate power trip. I've never had any other purpose in life. It's not exercise that's kept me going, but Jaya. She's the one I've tried to shape and hone into... into what? The ideal daughter? A useful member of society? A perfect wife? Oh God, what have I done? I think I'm going to be sick. IfeelsickIfeelsickIfeelsick. I feel...

the present – panic

My eyes flick open. I feel sick. I've lost perspective. Not metaphorically, but quite literally. From my horizontal position on Jaya's bed, I watch as her bedroom grows to monstrous proportions and the bed shrinks in terror. I close my eyes, but I can still feel the distorted vastness of the cavernous room beyond my eyelids. I disentangle myself from Jaya and get up from the bed. I feel as if I'm moving through a pool of sludge. I can all but see the slimy gunk pulsating around the room, lapping against the walls and surging up in great waves against my body; it restricts my movements, glues my eyelids together, coagulates in my mouth and fills my lungs so that I can barely breathe. I fight my way downstairs and collapse on the sofa, hyperventilating. I try yoga breathing, long deep exhalations, but ragged panting is all I can manage. I lose all feeling in my body, apart from at my very core, which radiates a deep and excruciating heat. My heart is breaking, bursting, exploding out of my chest. A million ruptured blood vessels spray the walls red. I see red. Everything is red, flashing and bloody, like gory fireworks. I think I must be dying.

Suddenly mum is beside me. She scoops me up in her strong arms and holds me tight while I twist and convulse. She strokes my hair and whispers in my ear, 'breathe, my darling. Just breathe.' Slowly the panic subsides. My breathing slows and the feeling returns to my benumbed limbs in an agonising blaze of pins and needles. Mum is crying. 'I'm sorry, I'm so sorry,' she says again and again. Her tears are hot and wet on my face. 'It's OK,' I tell her. 'I forgive you. I love you.' I open my eyes and smile at her, but she is not there. Instead I'm looking into the frightened eyes of my daughter.

PART FIVE
JAYA & JOHN

'Learn from yesterday, live for today, hope for tomorrow.'

Albert Einstein

new beginnings

John: It's the last day of term and the students have taken over college, running riot in their Santa hats and Christmas jumpers. As I wait to be summoned into Meeting Room 5, I'm unable to share in their festive joy. I stick my hand in my pocket and wrap it around my lucky Luke Skywalker figure, drawing strength from its familiar plastic contours. I wasn't expecting to be sitting here again after the last horrific meeting two days ago. Me and dad versus the Principal and a grim-faced policewoman. The Principal's words still ring in my ears:

'Never in all my years in Further Education have I been so disgusted by the behaviour of a college employee.'

I thought dad was going to kill him. 'You have absolutely no proof!' he roared, as if that would make any difference. The Principal wasn't interested in proving my guilt or innocence.

'This new allegation is immaterial,' he informed us. 'We have sufficient evidence to suggest that John's relationship with Miss Jones has been inappropriate.'

No prizes for guessing who provided the "evidence". Dad wanted me to bring Karen into it, but I didn't see the point in prolonging the agony. They wanted me gone and that was the end of it. Or so I thought until this morning's phone call.

Simon from HR sticks his head around the door.

'We're ready for you now, John.'

I try to swallow, but my throat is too dry. I follow him into the room and look around at the assembled group – Karen, Mandy, Simon – all smiling benevolently at me. Why is Karen smiling? Maybe the police have decided to arrest me after all? She'd love that.

'You're off the hook!' She beams at me as if it's the best news she's ever heard. 'Mrs Jones rang this morning. Jaya admitted to her that she made it all up. The kiss, the sexual encounter, it was all pure fabrication!'

'I told you that at the time, Karen.' Despite my intense relief, I can't quite keep the anger from my voice.

She nods, sagely. 'To be honest, I suspected as much myself,' she says, more to Mandy and Simon than to me.

'Did you?' I say. 'Because, as I recall you—'

'Please, John,' she laughs, darting nervous looks at her perplexed colleagues, 'let's not quibble over details. The main thing is, your reputation is restored and you'll be pleased to know you can return to work after Christmas.'

I don't even need to think about my response. 'No thanks.'

'Beg pardon?' I can't believe she's surprised. As if I would *ever* work with her again!

'I mean... I won't be resuming my post, Karen.'

'Right. OK. I quite understand.'

'You do?'

'Yes and I can't say I blame you', she sighs. 'Things would have been impossibly awkward between you and the students. Especially Jaya. Rest assured, we'll be having a stern word with the little madam this afternoon.'

'Oh, I'd quite happily work with *Jaya* again,' I say meaningfully.

She fixes me with a steely stare which clearly warns, *'Don't fuck with me!'* Our unspoken conversation has turned into outright war.

She stands. 'Well, we're all very sorry to see you go,' she says, extending her hand towards me.

Tell them, John! Tell them she offered to destroy Jaya's letter in exchange for sex. Tell them how she was coked-up to the eyeballs when she sexually harassed you and tried to bribe you into sleeping with her.

'Well, as I said, I don't have a problem with Jaya...' I lean back in my chair, enjoying Karen's discomfort as she's forced to sit back down. I look her directly in the eyes and she's suddenly beset by a mysterious coughing fit.

'Excuse me,' she gasps, hands flapping, eyes wide and vulnerable, 'it's my asthma.'

Damn she's good!

Mandy and Simon turn towards her, tutting and "ah"ing sympathetically. I feel like a player in a particularly challenging tennis match.

'Do you need to go home?' asks Simon. 'We could carry on the meeting without you?'

'No, I'm fine,' she says bravely, but there is real fear in her voice. I clear my throat and all eyes are now on me again.

'The way I see it,' I continue, 'Jaya just got herself in a bit of a muddle, that's all. After all, it's common for young girls to develop a crush on their teachers, isn't it? It must have taken her a lot of courage to admit the truth and she deserves praise for that, not punishment.'

Mandy and Simon nod and smile their approval.

Deuce!

'Well, I must say, that's very charitable of you,' says Simon. 'So, can I ask why you don't want to come back to work?'

189

I've fantasised about this very moment for weeks. The opportunity to finally get my own back on Karen. To let everyone at college know exactly what a corrupt, unprofessional, malicious little cow she is; to make her life as miserable as mine has been for the past few weeks. Maybe even to get her sacked? I look at Mandy and Simon, smiling expectantly at me and then slowly, I turn to look at Karen, squirming like the little worm she is. I could destroy her with the speech I've prepared.

Do it, John. Now's your chance!

I take a deep breath. 'I just think it's time to move on.'

As I walk out the college gates, I feel proud of myself for the first time in weeks. I could have hurt Karen, but it would have been cruel and pointless. The self-loathing has abated somewhat and I feel as if I've gone some way to redeeming myself. It's a good feeling. I don't know if Sarah will see things the same way, but if I don't try to convince her, I know I'll always regret it.

Go for it, John!

I walk straight from the college gates to the train station and buy a one-way ticket to London.

Jaya: Last night I dreamed about my dad. It's the first time I've ever dreamed about him and it was brilliant. He was tall and really good-looking and he had the same eyes as me, just like I always imagined. We were walking along the seashore holding hands and he was wearing floaty white clothes that billowed all around him. He looked a bit like an angel. I felt so happy to be with my dad but I felt sad too because in my heart I knew it was just a dream. He was looking out to sea and the wind was blowing his hair around his face. Then I noticed he was crying and I knew he was sad because of what I did to John. He was so upset that he couldn't look at me. He said I love you Jaya, but what you did was very wrong. You should never tell lies

190

about a person. I know daddy I told him. I'm sorry. Then he turned and smiled at me and I felt happy again. I'll never tell lies again I told him. Good girl said my dad and he hugged me. Then I asked him the question. The big question. The most important question in the world. Why did you never try to find me dad? I miss you every day. He looked very serious and he said I'm sorry baby I never meant to hurt you, but in real life I don't even know you exist. So I said life is much nicer in dreams don't you think? And then I began to cry. Then he said my poor baby and he kissed me on the forehead and wiped away my tears with a peacock feather. I don't know why he was holding a peacock feather but he was. Then all of a sudden he laughed and said peacock feather, peacock feather, PEACOCK FEATHER and then he turned into Kishan. Dreams are weird like that.

Me and mum went to college this afternoon because Karen wanted to speak to me. She told me John has decided not to come back to college even though I've told the truth about everything now. I'm glad I don't have to see him again. I don't think I could stand it now that I know for sure he doesn't love me. It's the last day before the holidays so I didn't have to go to any lessons but I saw all my friends in the cafeteria. Everyone was really nice to me, even Kerry Holt who isn't my friend any more. She told me she was sorry for all the horrible things she said and asked me to forgive her. I told her I'd think about it but I'll probably say yes because she is my best friend after all. When we went in to see Karen, she asked mum to wait outside for a few minutes and I was really scared that she was going to shout at me. But it actually turned out great because Karen asked me if I wanted to apply to do a Level One BTEC in Childcare. I told her I thought it might be too hard for me, but she said it would be a good progression route. I said I

191

thought she'd said that I couldn't go any higher at college, but she said I could get a support worker to help me with my work. I said I thought I'd been in too much trouble to stay on, but she said everyone deserves a second chance. I said I didn't know if my mum would say yes and she said for goodness sake Jaya, of course your mum will say yes because she wants what's best for you and don't you want this opportunity to develop and move on? And so I said OK I'll do it and now I can't wait. Karen called mum in and told her what she told me and mum was really happy. Mum and Karen had a long talk but I didn't really listen to what they were saying. Before we left, mum gave Karen a hug which was a bit weird because she never hugs anyone except for me and Bee. I think I'm going to like the course because I love babies and I know first aid and everything. One day I want to get married and have babies. But not just yet. First I want to get some qualifications under my belt. Then maybe a job. Then maybe I'll get married and have babies. Who knows what the future holds?

PART SIX
KISHAN

'Writing is my way out of a lonely place [...]
Autism is my prison, but typing is the air of freedom
and peace.'

Sarah Stup

kishan

I see the bird flying in the sky
flying so high in the sky
I cannot fly
but the bird flies in the sky
so high in the sky
People can't fly
But birds and planes and bees can

***

I wake up in the morning
mum is singing in the kitchen
she sings a nice song
wake me up before you go go
mum sings too loud
but I like to hear her sing
she sings a nice song
before you go go wake me up
I like to hear mum sing
when I wake up in the morning

***

Dudley Zoo
is full of animals
elephants and monkeys

and there's a castle too
Dudley Zoo
is full of animals
lions and tigers
and there's a castle too

***

Izzie talks like a lion
Loud roar
Jaya talks like a monkey
Chatter chatter
Mum talks like a river
Softly flowing
Mum's voice is best

***

I smile at the sun
it is warm on my face
I smile at the sun
as I sit in my garden
I watch ants on the grass
running up and down
they go back to their nest
and I smile at the sun

***

When I am on the minibus
going to the day centre
I see the clouds go by
and the trees go by
and the shops go by
and the people in the streets go by
The minibus smells of fish and chips
my favourite food

Dave the driver
wears a uniform
and a big smile on his face
Hello Kishan
When I am on the minibus
going to the day centre
I see the back of Dave's head
and hear music on the radio
Heart FM
When I am on the minibus
going to the day centre
I sit next to Kim Allen
I sit behind Sanjay Kumar
I sit in front of Rob Blake
We all have our own places
on the minibus
going to the day centre

***

hope

Izzie: She flings herself through my open front door and into my arms, eyes streaming with tears, nose bubbling with snot. Have I ever seen her cry before? I don't think so. I instinctively know it's something to do with Kishan. Nothing else would make Bee cry. I pray to God that he's OK.

'What is it, sweetie? Is something wrong with Kishan?' At the sound of his name, her wailing intensifies and my worst fears are confirmed.

'Oh God, Bee, is he hurt? Where is he?' I shake her by the shoulders. 'Speak to me, sweetheart, *please!*' She babbles something incomprehensible into my shoulder.

'What? I can't hear you, Bee!' She takes a deep breath and tries again.

'I said Kishan's fine.' She begins to giggle hysterically. 'Sort of.'

'Sort of? You're not making any sense!'

Her giggling turns back into demented sobbing.

'What the bloody hell is going on here, Bee?' I'm eventually forced to shout. She thrusts a damp, dog-eared exercise book into my hands.

'Read it,' she pants.

I open the book and glance at the first page. It contains a short poem, printed from a computer and then carefully cut out and stuck down with glue.

'Who wrote this?' I ask.

'Kishan,' she whispers.

I shake my head dumbly, uncomprehending. Thumbing through the book, I see that it is crammed full of Kishan's poetry. My hands are shaking so much as I begin to read, that I can barely keep the book still.

'Kishan? Kishan wrote all these?' I ask in wonder. Bee nods, wiping away more tears. I suddenly remember reading a story in the paper a few years ago about a non-verbal autistic girl in America writing the most beautiful stories and poems.

'Oh God, I've heard of this sort of thing happening before.'

'He's been writing them on the computer at the day centre,' says Bee, 'they thought I knew about it.' I throw back my head and let out a loud whoop.

'Bee, this is amazing, *incredible!*'

She nods, her eyes shining. 'I always knew my boy was in there somewhere, trying to communicate with the world.'

'Who knows,' I laugh, 'this could be the beginning of a distinguished writing career. He might even make his old mum rich.'

Bee grabs my hand and smiles at me. 'I already am rich,' she says.

As she clasps me to her breast, I pray that this is a sign of better times to come. For the first time since we met, there's hope for both our children. Can we finally look forward to a brighter future? For a brief moment, I succumb to a delicious shiver of anticipation, but I remind myself of the task ahead and shake it off.

'You OK?' asks Bee, feeling me tremble against her.

'Just emotional,' I tell her, which is also true. I extricate myself from her embrace and wipe away her tears with my palm.

'You off out?' she asks, noticing my handbag and umbrella by the door.

'Uh-huh – things to do, people to see and all that.'

She narrows her eyes at me. 'You're going to see him aren't you?'

I nod.

'Why?'

'Have to.'

'No you don't.'

'Oh, but I do.'

'What good will it do?'

'I'll tell you when I get back.'

She throws up her hands in mock despair, but nothing can dampen her good mood today. I'm so happy for her. For her and for Kishan. I kiss my best friend lightly on the cheek and step out into the cold winter sunshine.

PART SEVEN
IZZIE & RICHARD

'It is not time or opportunity that is to determine intimacy; it is disposition alone. Seven years would be insufficient to make some people acquainted with each other, and seven days are more than enough for others.'

Jane Austen

coup de foudre

Izzie: I got his address from Jaya. She knows where he lives, his phone number, his date of birth and a whole host of other personal details. I don't know whether to be proud or appalled by her skills as a super-sleuth/stalker. All morning I've been asking myself if I'm doing the right thing, but I just can't leave things the way they are. I rehearse my little speech under my breath: 'John, I want to tell you how sorry I am for all the pain and suffering Jaya and I have caused you. Please believe me, there was never any malicious intent on either of our parts. I hope you can find it in your heart to forgive us.' No matter how many times I repeat it, it does nothing to ease my nerves.

Jaya wanted to come with me, but I told her I didn't think it was a good idea. 'I just want to say sorry too,' she said, her eyes brimming with tears. I didn't realise she was capable of such heart-felt remorse, but I'm starting to see that she has many qualities for which I've never before given her credit. That awful night, I think I might have died if she hadn't found me. She was so tender, so competent. Not like Jaya at all. It was a revelation. She nursed me through the night, gave me a paper bag to breathe into, mopped my fevered brow and sat with me while I slept. Did I ever really know her at all until that night? I've always been so wrapped up in her, but it's hardly the same thing. I

203

know that I see her as special and different, but maybe that's wrong of me. I always thought that I accepted her for who she is, but now I'm not so sure. "Acceptance" and "tolerance", "equality" and "diversity"; the buzzwords of the liberal and the fair. What do these terms even mean? Maybe I've been so preoccupied with "accepting" what I see to be her limitations and deficiencies, that I've been blind to her natural abilities, her innate "*Jayaness*", the unique and beautiful qualities that make her truly special.

Richard: Alice has gone. She's cleared out her half of the wardrobe, cleared out the joint bank account and cleared out of my life. The "Dear John" letter she left on the kitchen table *was* for John. Nothing for me, not even a text. John doesn't know yet. He's in London with Sarah. It seems their relationship is salvageable, in spite of everything. She's a nice girl and I'm happy for him. Of course, he'll be upset when he comes home, but he's been expecting it. Anyway, I'm sure we'll be just fine on our own. We're quite good mates now, John and I. And I – I feel great! After weeks and months of dreading this day, it's a relief to finally get it over with. If I'm honest I feel lighter, elated even, as if I've been relieved of a huge burden. I even found myself singing in the shower this morning, which is a particularly strange way to react to the end of one's marriage. Either I've had a complete emotional breakdown, but it hasn't hit me yet, or: I'm actually happy.

Izzie: I can hear him humming softly to himself as he opens the front door.

'John,' I begin, desperate to get my apology out as quickly as possible and then get the hell out of here, 'I'm sorry to turn up like this, but I want to tell you how...' I trail off. The man in front of me is definitely not John. Admittedly, he's tall and good-looking, just as Jaya

204

described, but he's about forty-five years old and his hair is dark, not blond.

'Are you John's father?' I ask him.

'I do have that dubious honour,' he replies, a curious smile forming at the corners of his mouth. 'And you are?'

'Jaya's mum,' I say, tense and woolly-mouthed.

'Ah.' The smile disappears. 'John's not here. He's gone to London.' I feel desperately disappointed, but I can't quite work out why.

'I wanted to apologise,' I say.

'Right. Well, you'd better come in then.'

Richard: And suddenly, like a bolt from the blue, like an angel from heaven, on the very day my wife leaves me, unbelievably, incredibly, magically, the most beautiful woman I have ever seen appears on my doorstep. I take one look at her and my heart leaps out of my chest. I've never been a great believer in love at first sight, but at this particular moment, I'm struggling to come up with an alternative explanation. She said she's Jaya's mother, although she doesn't seem old enough. That threw me for a minute. I panicked, invited her in, desperate for an excuse to keep her here a little while longer. This is hardly a promising start to things, yet I know, without a shadow of a doubt, that I want to be with this woman.

fate

Izzie: I'm not sure why he invited me in and I haven't a clue why I agreed, as I had every intention of making a hasty getaway. Yet here I am, in his living room, accepting a weak-looking cup of tea and coughing nervously as I drink it. I'm suddenly aware that he's staring at me. I look up and he's fixing me with a gaze so intense that I'm suddenly struck by the stupidity of entering a strange man's house, alone, especially when the man in question has every reason to hate me.

'You must hate me,' I say, testing the waters.

He smiles and shakes his head – clearly a man of few words, but at least he doesn't seem to mean me any harm. A picture on the mantelpiece behind him catches my eye – a framed photograph of my host in uniform. He follows my gaze.

'I'm in... I mean I was in the police force,' he explains.

I relax a little. If he was a policeman, then he's unlikely to bash my brains in and bury me in the back garden. I hope.

Richard: She is simply stunning. Long, red hair, pinned up loosely at the back. A square, handsome face, which is both strong and vulnerable. Huge blue eyes. The body of a Greek Goddess, with the mere hint of Roman Gladiator thrown in for good measure. Dressed simply in an assortment of soft, woolly and embroidered fabrics, which cling gently to her curves. Shabby chic, it suits her beautifully.

Izzie: He's not said a word in five minutes. He's just sitting there, looking at me. Strangely, even though we've never met before, I don't feel intimidated. His gaze is gentle and appraising, as if he's known me for years and is admiring a new outfit or haircut. Still, enough is enough. Putting down my cup, I look up and meet his eyes, raising my eyebrow questioningly.

Richard: It's the arched eyebrow that did it. Quite possibly the most beautiful arched eyebrow I've ever seen. I was about to say something, break the silence, amaze her with my conversational prowess, when she looked at me and raised her eyebrow. It rendered me speechless... tongue-tied and stupid. Now I can't take my eyes off her. If only I could think of something intelligent to say.

Izzie: Well that didn't work out quite the way I planned. I thought my questioning look would end the silence, but instead it's only intensified it. Now we're both openly staring at each other, which, any moment now, will start to get ridiculously awkward.

'Is this a competition?' I ask, 'because, if it is, I must warn you that I'm a local staring contest champion.'

He chuckles. It is warm, throaty and immensely gratifying. I'm suddenly struck by the realisation that I want to hear that sound again. Many, many more times. The thought makes me blush and, flustered, I drop my gaze.

'I win,' he says softly and I begin to giggle uncontrollably.

Richard: She's laughing now and the sound is as sweet and pleasurable as any I've ever heard. I smile back at her, like the cat who got the cream, basking in the sunshine of her laughter.

Izzie: 'So,' I ask him, 'do you usually invite strange women in just to stare at them?'

'I'm sorry,' he replies, 'it's just that I find you impossibly beautiful.' His answer seems to take us both by surprise.

'Oh,' is all I can manage in reply.

Richard: I've blown it, I know I have! I've said too much, too soon. I'm no bloody good at this, always seem to say the wrong thing. Any minute now she's going to walk out of my house, like any sensible person would, and I'll never see her again. The thought makes me bold. I take a deep breath and lean in towards her.

'I know this is wildly inappropriate, but could I please take you out for dinner tonight?'

She narrows her eyes at me and juts out her chin. 'And what about your son?'

'My son?' I repeat, moronically.

'My daughter falsely accused him of sexual assault, *if you remember.*' She's clearly irritated by my apparent lack of paternal feeling.

'Of course I remember. John's been through hell.'

'So can I ask why you want to take me out for dinner?' she asks, more confused than angry. 'After all, I'm the person who called the police and got him sacked from his job.'

I decide that total honesty is my only option. 'Look, all I know is that when I saw you standing on my door-step just now, it gave me a feeling of intense joy, the first moment of real happiness I've experienced in a very long time. I asked you in because I couldn't bear to see you walk away and now that you're here, I can't bear the thought of never seeing you again. I don't know why you make me feel like this, but I just have to find out. So please, *please* will you have dinner with me tonight?'

Izzie: I must be dreaming. In real life, handsome, sexy, intelligent strangers do *not* fall at your feet and beg you to go out with them. Any minute now I'll wake up and, and, he's looking at me so intensely that I can't think straight. His eyes are pleading, *desperate* and his vulnerability makes me dizzy with desire. Oh God what should I do? How can I say yes? What kind of a mother would I be? He's John's *father* for crying out loud! I could hardly keep his identity a secret from Jaya. Besides, he's clearly married. A fat gold band gleams ostentatiously on his finger and his glamorous wife stares accusingly at me from a framed wedding photo on the wall. Admittedly, he may be divorced, or even widowed, but even so, do I really want to embark upon a relationship with a man who would put his own desires ahead of his son's happiness? Then again, I definitely feel something for this man. I'm not sure if it's love or lust, or if I've just been bowled over by his good looks and passionate words, but either way, don't I owe it to myself to find out? OK. I really need to answer him now. So what do I say? Oh God, what do I say, what do I say, what do I say?

Richard: By the look on her face, I'd say she's struggling to decide if becoming involved with me is worth the inevitable problems it will bring. I feel guilty that I'm not doing more soul-searching myself, but after years of living in an emotional and sexual wasteland, I'm letting my heart lead on this one. Besides, I'm convinced that fate has brought us together today and who am I to argue against fate?

getting acquainted

Richard: She's here! I didn't think she'd come, but she's *actually* here. I wish I hadn't had that double whiskey now, but I really didn't think she'd turn up. She looks sensational. I knew I should have suggested somewhere a bit more upmarket. But then again, this place is intimate and friendly. Somewhere where we can really get to know each other. OK, she's coming over. She looks *so* beautiful. I can't believe I've only just noticed what incredible breasts she has. Bloody hell, Richard, you must really be smitten if you didn't even check out her tits! Oh for goodness sake, get your mind out of the gutter. This is the woman you want to spend the rest of your life with. You need to seduce her with your rakish charm and scintillating conversation, not gawp at her chest all night. OK, she's seen me and she's coming over. Stop. Looking. At. Her. Breasts.

Izzie: I can't believe it! He's quite unashamedly checking out my breasts!

Richard: Shit! She's noticed me looking at her breasts. As she joins me at the bar, she eyes me quizzically, but thankfully doesn't mention my huge faux pas.

'I didn't think you'd come,' I say.

'Yeah, sorry I'm late,' she replies, 'I wasn't sure if I was coming myself.' She smiles and I feel instantly better.

'You find a table,' I tell her, 'I'll get you a drink. What would you like?'

'A large glass of red, please. Looks like I've got some catching up to do.'

She smiles again. A good sign. Still, I keep a close eye on her as she saunters off across the crowded bar, just in case she changes her mind and runs off into the night.

Izzie: I take the opportunity to study him from across the room. Tall, muscular, a slight limp, probably an old injury received in the line of duty. Dark hair with a smattering of grey at the temples. Confident, but not overly so. There's a certain sadness about him which I can't quite put my finger on. He turns from the bar and heads towards the table, clutching a bottle of wine and two glasses. As he gets nearer I can see that the hand holding the wine bottle is shaking and that his forehead is damp and shiny. It occurs to me that he's just as nervous as I am and the realisation helps me to relax a little.

'So are you a korma or a vindaloo kind-of-girl?' he asks as he sits down. I hesitate momentarily as I consider my answer, which is enough to send him into a major panic. 'Oh God, you do like curry don't you?' he whimpers.

'Of course,' I reassure him. He still looks worried and so I add, with my brightest, most convincing smile, 'I love curry!'

'Are you sure?' he asks. 'Shall we have a drink here and then go somewhere else?'

'No. I like it here,' I tell him, 'and I genuinely *do* like Indian food. I picked up a few recipes when I was out there and I do a lot of authentic Asian cooking at home.'

'You've been to India?' He seems surprised. Then the penny drops. 'Of course, Jaya's mixed race, isn't she? Is that where you met her father?' I nod, not wanting to elaborate.

211

'Well, I love this restaurant,' he says, 'the beer's cold, the waiters are friendly and the food is *amazing*.' He smiles at me and I smile back, grateful to him for the swift change of topic.

Richard: She seems reluctant to talk about Jaya's father. I wonder how well she knew him. Was he a holiday romance or a long-term boyfriend? Maybe they were married. She might have gone out to India to be with him. Or perhaps she didn't know him at all. Not that it matters, of course. It's just that I'm intrigued by this woman. I find myself wanting to know everything there is to know about her.

'So tell me about Jaya,' I venture. She immediately stiffens.

'Why do you want to talk about Jaya?' she asks.

'I don't know. I'm just interested, I suppose.' She looks away, refusing to meet my eye. I take her hand across the table.

'Look, I just want to get to know you, that's all. I thought Jaya might be a good starting point.' She softens and nods.

'Sorry, I'm just a bit defensive. Because of what Jaya did to John. I was so angry with her, but I can't stand anyone else criticising her.'

I hold up my hands. 'Hey, I wasn't going to criticise her!'

She hangs her head. 'You would have every right to,' she says quietly.

'I'm not here to judge your daughter. I know she has special needs.' She stiffens again. 'Sorry, isn't that the PC term any more?'

'She has a mild learning difficulty,' she sniffs.

'OK, fine, whatever. What I'm trying to say is that she just made a mistake and it's all forgotten about now.'

212

'Really?' she asks.

'Of course. John's not the type of lad to hold any grudges. Anyway, I think he feels bit guilty himself.' She looks up at me, wide-eyed.

'Whatever for?'

'Well,' I hesitate. The last thing I want to do is point the finger of blame back at John. 'Between you and me, I don't think he received the proper training on how to deal with young ladies with spec... with learning difficulties.' She is immediately alert, eyeing me keenly.

'So you're saying the college is at fault for what happened?'

'Well, I wouldn't say that, exactly. I just feel that, as a young lad fresh out of university, he could perhaps have done with a bit more guidance.'

She purses her lips. 'So why does John feel guilty?' she asks. I begin to shift uncomfortably in my seat, torn between my loyalty to my son and my desire to answer her honestly.

'Look, John was only ever friendly towards Jaya,' I assure her, 'but he should really have read the signs earlier. He didn't see that she had a crush on him until it was too late. I think, with hindsight, he wishes he'd have put a bit more professional distance between the two of them, to avoid any confusion about their relationship.'

For some reason, my answer seems to bring her great pleasure and she leans back in her chair with a satisfied smile. I feel suddenly oddly ecstatic that I've brought a smile to her face, although the exact cause and nature of the smile elude me. I reciprocate and we sit for a few moments grinning at each other.

Izzie: I feel as if a weight has been lifted from my shoulders. He's helped me see things from a whole new perspective. Now that I know about John's lack of experience and training, I can see how he might have given Jaya the wrong impression. Of course, she should never have lied, but she may genuinely have believed John was her boyfriend. Knowing Jaya, she would have spun an intricate web of alternative truths in her head and may have struggled to emotionally extricate herself. I'm so thankful that he's helped me see things from Jaya's point-of-view that I lean across the table and place my hand on his.

'Thank you,' I say.

Richard: 'What for?' I ask, surprised and delighted by her sudden closeness and unexpected warmth.

She sighs. 'I was so upset when Jaya told me she'd lied about John. When I asked her why she'd done such a terrible thing, she told me that she'd *wanted* it to be true – as if that explained everything.' Her voice wavers and I wait while she composes herself. She looks up at me and there are tears in her eyes. This is clearly an emotional subject for her. I smile in what I hope to be an encouraging "please go on" sort of way, but all I can think about is how beautiful her eyes are, brimming and shimmering with tears. She takes a sip of wine before continuing. 'I was just so disappointed in her,' she sighs. 'I thought I'd brought her up better than that. It felt like a personal failing. Do you know what I mean?' She looks at me for confirmation and I rack my brain for a suitably soothing response.

'Every parent knows that feeling,' I eventually settle upon.

She smiles, clearly grateful. 'I've never known her to tell an outright lie before,' she continues. 'I know she can get confused at times, but this was different. It seemed so deliberate and premeditated.'

I nod, holding her gaze as she pauses to drain her glass. 'More wine?' I ask.

She shakes her head and covers the rim with her elegant fingers, but then suddenly changes her mind with a cheeky "what the hell" roll of her eyes.

Izzie: 'So you felt hurt? Let down?' he probes, as he refills my glass.

'I suppose,' I sigh, 'but it went deeper than that.' I don't elaborate. I've probably said too much already. How much more do I want to open up to him? I look him in the eyes. They are full of compassion and concern. I feel so comfortable talking to him, but maybe I'm being a bit over familiar for a first date. 'Sorry,' I say, 'I'm sure you don't want to hear about my problems.'

'Believe me, I do,' he replies, so earnestly that I'm a little taken aback.

'Why?' I ask, intrigued.

'Easy question,' he laughs. 'Number one,' he begins to tick off the reasons on his fingers, 'I like the sound of your voice. Number two, I want to help you if I can and number three, when I'm listening to your problems, I'm not thinking about my own.'

'Good reasons,' I concede. 'So, shall we move on to your problems next?'

'Perhaps not,' he replies, 'you'd walk straight out of here if I told you half of what's been going on in my life recently.' For a moment he looks sad, almost wistful, but then he gives me his cute lopsided grin. 'Let's just stick to you for the time-being, eh?'

I shrug. 'It's been a difficult few weeks, that's all,' I tell him, honestly. 'My daughter is the most important person in my life and I love her with all my heart. I went a little crazy when I thought she'd been abused and so when she told me she'd made it all up, I just felt... numb. I couldn't get my head around why she'd done it, but I felt that, somehow, somewhere I was partly to blame.'

215

He shakes his head vehemently. 'You shouldn't blame yourself,' he says, 'who knows what goes on in kids' heads?' He smiles, ruefully. 'I haven't got a clue what John's thinking half the time.'

'No,' I insist, 'there are a lot of things I wish I'd done differently...' I trail off because some things are best left unsaid, especially to an (almost) complete stranger. 'Let's just say I've done some things I'm not proud of.'

'Haven't we all?' he says, gently. I look at him. In his eyes I see that same wistful look I saw earlier. I imagine those eyes locked on mine as we make love and I shiver. He notices and raises his eyebrows. I smile briskly.

'Well, you've helped me feel a whole lot better,' I conclude, 'so thank you.'

Richard: 'You're welcome,' I reply. She looks so sexy, sitting there smiling shyly at me from under her lashes. Would it be inappropriate to tell her that I want her? I gulp down my wine as I ponder the question. 'YES', says my brain. 'I want you,' says my mouth.

'Wh-at!?' says the beautiful woman sitting opposite me. The intimate atmosphere of the last hour is destroyed and I realise with dismay that a heroic effort will be required on my part to salvage the situation. I make a desperate grab for her hand.

'Look, you *must* feel it too! The French call it *coup de foudre*, literally translated it means a lightning bolt, but we call it—'

'Love at first sight.' She completes my sentence and is now looking at me the way John does when he thinks I'm being a patronising old fart. Of course she speaks French, she's my ideal woman, so it stands to reason that she should speak French. Shit. My ardent declaration of love isn't quite going according to plan. I try to think of something

216

complimentary to say, something to divert attention from my bumbling foolishness.

'You look fucking fantastic tonight!'

She gasps, her exquisite lips forming an astonished "o". I'm so captivated by the open-mouthed sensuality of her appearance, that it takes me a few seconds to realise that she's probably more horrified than turned on. I quickly swap my maniacal grin for what I hope to be a more acceptable "first-date" facial expression and clear my throat.

'Forgive me. I'm nervous and drunk and, and I just fancy the pants off you.'

Izzie: I don't know whether to laugh or cry. He's like a completely different person to the attentive companion of five minutes ago. Maybe it was all just a ploy to impress and seduce me? He says he's nervous, but I've got a sneaking suspicion that I'm seeing the real him. But in spite of (or maybe even because of!) his vulgarity and pompousness, I'm finding myself increasingly attracted to him. He's so unlike anyone I've ever met before. He's fascinating and complex and *exciting*! I decide to put the poor guy out of his misery.

'Just shut up and kiss me!'

Richard: Our lips meet and everything in the world makes sense.

Izzie: This is the most incredible, amazing, beautiful thing that has ever happened to me! It's *everything* the books and films want you to believe. It really does feel and sound like fireworks and harps and violins and explosions! I feel alive and on fire and electrically charged and all the other wonderful clichés associated with this marvellous, life-affirming feeling!

We pull apart and he throws back his head and "woo-hoos" like a teenage boy. And then we're laughing and kissing and touching, making a spectacle of ourselves there and then in the restaurant. He pulls away from me, suddenly.

'So, what now?' he asks.

'What do you mean?' My head is spinning. I can barely focus on his words.

'Do we keep it casual, or move in together, or what?' He's breathless, laughing. I think about it for a few seconds.

'I know what I want right now,' I say.

Richard: She looks at me suddenly with such unmistakable desire that I'm filled with reciprocal lust, which is so intense, it's excruciating. But before I make a complete arse of myself, I have to check.

'I'm sorry to ask, but do you mean sex?' She giggles and looks away, coyly. 'Only, I have to make sure, because I have been known to misread the signals in the past.'

'Yes, I do mean sex,' she laughs.

I push back my chair and it clatters to the ground. I throw a handful of notes on the table, grab her hand and we run out of the restaurant, sniggering and giggling and hugging and stumbling like schoolchildren.

love

Izzie: I take a deep breath and luxuriate in his smell, an intoxicating scent of coriander and cologne. I've been here before; an outline moving in the shadows, a supple and angular body, a hungry mouth on my neck, a vibration on my ankle. A vibration on my ankle? Bugger! My mobile! My mobile's ringing in my trouser pocket down by my feet.

'Don't answer it,' he murmurs in my ear.

'It might be Jaya,' I say, pushing him off me. I grab my phone. It's Jaya.

'Hi mum.' I can tell she's been crying.

'What's wrong? Where's Bee?'

'She's downstairs watching TV. I can't sleep.'

'Why not?'

'I was thinking about you. And about my dad.'

'Your dad?!'

'I keep dreaming about him.'

'You've been dreaming about...your dad?' Jaya hasn't mentioned her father in over ten years.

'Where are you?' she asks.

I sneak a guilty look at the gorgeous, naked man next to me, doing his best to pretend he's not listening to my conversation.

'I'm on my way home,' I say.

Richard: This is not good. Not good at all. She puts down her mobile and turns to me.

'I'm sorry. I can't do this.'

'Yes you can!' I almost yell. I take her hands in mine. 'You can, you can, you can!'

'I can't.' She pulls on her blouse and begins to do up the buttons.

'Stop! Please stop,' I beg. She stops and shakes her head sadly.

'Don't you see? I can't do this to Jaya!' Her eyes are huge, imploring. 'How can I have a relationship with *you* of all people? What if things get serious between us? What would I say to her? I just can't do it.'

'Just hear me out, will you? You owe me that, at least!' She shrugs, which I seize upon as a sign that she's open to negotiation. I grasp her by the shoulders and fix her squarely in the eyes.

'Don't you realise what a once-in-a-lifetime piece of good fortune this is? It's a never to be repeated chance to be happy. We owe it to ourselves to do something about it!' Her body slackens and her shoulders go limp between my palms. 'All I'm asking for is one more date. One more chance to get to know each other.' She begins to sob and I know I have to keep talking. 'Come away with me. This weekend. Just the two of us. If you still feel the same way after that, then, fine, you never have to see me again. Come on? What do you say?'

'I say...' Her words are no louder than a whisper escaping from her pale, trembling lips. I have to press my ear almost to her mouth to hear her.

'Yes?' I take her hands in mine.

'I say... what about John?'

'I don't want to think about John right now!' I explode, pushing her away from me and escaping to the other end of the bed. She shuffles along until we're sitting side-by-side again and her hand seeks out mine once more. We sit in silence, hands intertwined, lost in our mutual torment.

'Do you think he'd ever forgive you?' she continues eventually. 'And what would John and Jaya be to each other? Brother and sister? Can you *really* see us all playing happy families together?' I know she's right, but I just don't care.

'Don't do this,' I beg, 'don't sacrifice your happiness.'

She shrugs. 'I've done it before.'

'Well don't sacrifice mine, then!' I fling myself to my knees in front of her in a last-ditch attempt to win her over. 'This weekend. *Please* say yes.'

Her eyes are saying 'yes', her body's saying 'yes', so when she opens her mouth to speak, I hope against hope that she'll say '*yes*'.

'I'm sorry, but my answer's no.' My heart contracts painfully in my chest.

'Why?'

'You know why,' she says, gently.

'No, I mean why would fate play such a cruel trick? To bring you to me, knowing that I can't have you? Why? Today of all days.'

'What do you mean?'

I almost tell her about Alice, after all, it doesn't matter now. But I don't. I would hate her to think that my feelings towards her are anything other than genuine. She'd never believe me that I feel nothing for my wife and that I've fallen head-over-heels in love with her. Even though I'll probably never see her again, I need her to know that I love her. And that is why I place a gentle kiss on her lips and say three words that I've not said to anyone in a long, long time.

Izzie: As our lips part, I open my eyes.

221

'I love you,' he says.

Tears spring to my eyes and, in that moment, I know without a shadow of a doubt that I love him too.

'I have to go,' I say.

He doesn't try to stop me and accompanies me to the door of the hotel room in silence. I turn to him in the doorway.

'I wish things could be different.'

He looks at me with such immense sadness that I refrain from further platitudes. But there is just one thing I need to know before I walk out of his life forever.

'Can I ask you a question?'

He nods. 'Anything.'

'What's your name?' I ask.

Richard: I'd smile if I had any feeling left in my body.

'Richard. And yours?'

'Isabel.'

'Good-bye, Isabel.'

'Good-bye, Richard.'

Richard: And with that she is gone. I sit on the bed and surrender to the nothingness. Then calmly, I pick up my wallet and keys from the bedside cabinet. Calmly, I put on my coat and walk out of the same door she passed through five minutes earlier. Calmly, I go to the front desk and pay what I owe. Calmly, I walk to my car, bleep it open and climb inside. And then I'm calm no longer. Then I'm weeping and howling, screaming and smashing my fists against the steering wheel, gnashing my teeth and biting my snot-covered hands. Never in my life have I experienced such an outpouring of grief. All the bitter disappointment and hurt and heartache that I should have felt when my wife left me, is now being felt for a woman I've known for only a few hours. I let my anguish run its course. Eventually my tears subside and I regain sufficient composure to contemplate the empty wilderness that is my life. What now? How will I ever be able to move on from this? Is this the beginning or the end?

Izzie: I am awoken by the sound of gentle snoring and, for the brief moment before I open my eyes, I think I'm back in the hotel with Richard. But in my heart I know who is beside me. My daughter. Just as she has always been. It is her rightful place. I turn towards Jaya and smooth back the hair from her sleeping face. It's been years since she last climbed into bed with me. I push back the covers, careful not to wake her and creep downstairs to the kitchen. Dawn is breaking over Netherton, illuminating the wild scrubland at the back of our house. I make myself a strong black coffee and take it into the backyard. I take a huge gulp of good, honest Black Country air. My limbs slacken and a frisson goes through my body. There and then, I make a resolution, a promise to myself, which has nothing to do with Richard or what happened between us last night.

Nineteen years ago I gave life to Jaya and, in doing so, I relinquished my own. I realise now that it was wrong of me. If there's one thing the last few weeks have taught me, it's that I need to get my life back. God knows I love my daughter. Over the years, my love for Jaya has been my one and only solace; it got me through the loneliness and boredom of being a young single mum, it soothed my troubled mind when sleep deprivation threatened my sanity, it settled my rumbling belly when I could only afford to feed one of us and it provided me with comfort throughout all the daily trials and agonies of raising a child with learning difficulties. But the love one feels for one's child, no matter how powerful and all-consuming, should never be allowed to smother and extinguish one's own self. This is the mistake I made. For nineteen years, I've lived, breathed, slept and dreamed Jaya. It's time for me to bring back Izzie.

Epilogue

jaya 2020

Mum will be here soon. I'm all packed and ready. Two new nighties, my wash bag and all the pretty, soft pink things that Granny and Grandpa bought. Colin has been fussing around me all morning, but I just need a bit of time on my own. He's been really sweet and I love him so much, but I think he's more nervous than me. I hope he doesn't come back from his bike ride just yet. Maybe he'll go down to the reservoir – I know he loves it there. He reckons one day he'll buy a boat and call it Princess Jaya, but I'd rather spend the money on a caravan by the sea. Or even better, we could use it to get married on a beach in Goa. Mum would love that. She's never been back and I know she wants to. Yes – that's what we'll do.

I look out of the window and put my hand on my big smooth peach of a tummy. I wonder if I'll want to go back to the school afterwards? I think so. I'd really miss it otherwise and I'd miss the children too. It's been so much fun helping the little ones with their letters and numbers. Mrs Jenkins says I'm the best volunteer they've ever had. I think I'll make a good teaching assistant one day.

My tummy goes really stiff. What's that called again? Braxton Hicks. It means my body's getting ready for labour. Braxton Hicks don't really hurt, they just feel a bit tight and uncomfortable. Maybe that means labour won't hurt too much. I hope so. I do my breathing like the midwife showed me, thinking about the word "relax". As I breathe in I think "re" and as I breathe out, I think "lax". I try to keep my mind focused on the two syllables and keep my breathing in rhythm with them. I breathe in through my nose and out through my mouth, keeping my mouth soft and squashy as I breathe out. I stroke my beautiful baby through my own skin and I feel a tiny foot. I try to grab it but she kicks out and the foot moves to another place inside me. Soon my special little girl will be here. Everything is as it should be.

About The Author

Tanya Bullock is a college lecturer, writer and award-winning filmmaker. She lives in the West Midlands with her husband and two young children. She has a passion for foreign culture and languages (inherited from her French mother) and, in her youth, travelled extensively throughout Australia, America, Asia and Europe. As a filmmaker, she has gained local recognition, including funding and regional television broadcast, through ITV's *First Cut* scheme; two nominations for a Royal Television Society Midlands Award, and, in 2010, a Royal Television Society Award in the category of best promotional film. In 2008, she directed a short drama, *Second Honeymoon*, which was screened at the Cannes Film Festival. On maternity leave in 2011 and in need of a creative outlet, Tanya began to write this, her first novel, *That Special Someone*.

http://tanyabullock.wordpress.com/
https://www.facebook.com/tanyabullockwriter
Twitter: @TanyaBullock15

Keep up to date with all Tanya's news and new titles, join the Tanya Bullock Mailing List
http://eepurl.com/O_cjj
(All email details are securely managed at Mailchimp.com and are never, ever shared with third parties.)

Acknowledgements

Thank you to Dad for being a wonderful writer and storyteller and for inspiring me to follow in your footsteps. Thank you to Maman for our frequent conversations which have helped to shape and define my ideas. Thank you to you both for a childhood full of books, laughter, great conversation and togetherness. Merci – je vous aime infiniment.

Thank you to my brother and best friend Marc for the emotional support and for giving me your laptop, without which this book would never have been written. Thank you to my brother and best friend Dave for being my loudest and proudest supporter. You are both the very best of Bobs and I love you so much.

Thank you to my great friend Kaush for sharing in all my creative dreams.

Thank you to Kishan for lending me your name.

Thank you to Sarah, Emma, Rina, Luce, Catherine and Shev for being such brilliant friends. An extra thank you to Sarah for your faith in me and for telling me to 'go for it!' I'm so glad I took your advice.

Thank you to my friends Liz, Dilusha and Cath for your support and encouragement with the book.

Thank you to Emma Rose Millar for reading an early draft of the book and for giving me such positive feedback and encouragement.

Thank you to Catherine and John D for answering my questions and for being so kind and helpful.

Thank you to all my family and friends for sharing in my happiness; most especially Ishani, Ariane, Sohini,

Stuart, Margaret, Colette, Alain, Paul, Paula, Matthew, Megan, Kim, Adam, Alan, Carla, Josh, Morfydd, Rosemin, Rachel, Ronnie, Kate, Katie H, Michelle, Mary, Susie, Jen, Bev, Sadie, Katie F, Lauren, Trudi, Claire, Angie, Dave and Jo. (I must also mention here my tiny nieces and nephew who are too young to read my book but whom I love very much: Maya, Amelia, Alice, Daytona and Jenson).

Thank you to my cousin Nicky for helping me decide at an early age what I wanted to do in life.

Thank you to Stephanie Zia and Elle Ford for the invaluable editorial support, advice and words of wisdom. Thank you most of all for believing in me and for giving me back my self-belief. I am immensely grateful to you both.

Thank you to my husband Darren for giving me the space, time, love and support I need to be able to write. I love you.

Thank you to Katia and Jake for giving me the essential experience needed to write about motherhood. You have turned my world upside down and filled it with happiness. I love you both more than you will ever know.

More Blackbird Digital Titles

If this book has lived up to your expectations, please would
you consider leaving a review? Amazon.com for US or
Amazon.co.uk for UK? A couple of lines is plenty. It really
makes all the difference to us small independent publishers
who rely on word of mouth to get our books known. Thank
you!

Blackbird Digital Books
London

We publish rights-reverted and new titles by established
quality authors alongside exciting new talent

http://blackbird-books.com
@blackbirdebooks

Lightning Source UK Ltd.
Milton Keynes UK
UKOW04f2132041215

264045UK00002B/17/P

9 780993 307 0